# Tropi

Zoe Chant
© 2019 Zoe Chant
All Rights Reserved

# Shifting Sands Resort

This is book 9 of the Shifting Sands Resort series. All of my books are standalones (No cliffhangers! Always a happy ending!) and can be read independently, but many of these characters reappear in subsequent books, and there is a series arc. I suggest reading in order:
Tropical Tiger Spy (Book 1)
Tropical Wounded Wolf (Book 2)
Tropical Bartender Bear (Book 3)
Tropical Lynx's Lover (Book 4)
Tropical Dragon Diver (Book 5)
Tropical Panther's Penance (Book 6)
Tropical Christmas Stag (Book 7)
Tropical Leopard's Longing (Book 8)
Tropical Lion's Legacy (Book 9)
Tropical Dragon's Destiny (Book 10)

The Master Shark's Mate (A Fire & Rescue Shifters/Shifting Sands Resort crossover, occurs in the timeline between *Tropical Wounded Wolf* and *Tropical Bartender Bear*)
Firefighter Phoenix (A Fire & Rescue Shifters novel, has scenes set at Shifting Sands Resort, and occurs in the timeline between *Tropical Christmas Stag* and *Tropical Leopard's Longing*)

# Chapter 1

"YOU'VE GOT A VISITOR," the secretary told Alice Anders as she waltzed in the office to check her inbox. "I just paged you. He's waiting for you in the principal's office."

"Am I in trouble?" Alice asked archly.

To her surprise, the secretary only shook her head, looking flustered, and gestured at the principal's door even more anxiously.

Leafing through her pile of fundraiser fliers and dress code memos, Alice opened the door absently, and drew up short.

Sitting in Principal Wetch's seat was an undeniably impressive figure.

At six foot four inches tall, Alice was used to towering over other women, and even many men. But when this man stood politely when she entered the room, she had to look up to meet his eyes, and his shoulders were proportionally broad. His suit, probably worth twice Alice's middle-school gym teacher salary, did nothing to hide the fact that he was incredibly ripped. His brisk handshake was strong and he was dead handsome, with a strong, clean-shaven jaw and an artistic touch of gray in his short, dark hair.

Alice would have eaten her dirty gym socks if he wasn't a shifter and her bear rumbled in cautious agreement.

"Can I help you?" Alice asked, sitting across from him at his imperious gesture. She started to sit gingerly, then slouched deliberately.

"I think you can," he said in a silky voice, settling into the principal's seat and leaning back. "I understand you'll be traveling just after the end of the semester for your coworker's wedding."

"Yeeeeees," Alice said, drawing out the word. "Is there some problem with that? I should have my grades done in plenty of time. I'm only a gym teacher." She could not quite keep the challenge out of her voice; she never backed down from a fight and she sensed that this would shortly become one.

He smiled at her. "You're a bear shifter." It wasn't a question.

Alice froze, and could not help glancing at the door, still barely ajar. Shifters were a well-kept secret in this area.

Before she could formulate a response to his statement, he went on. "You have a brother in Oregon, and two aging parents here in Lakefield."

He gave her a conspiratorial look. "Such a shame that they'll be losing the house."

He continued before Alice could so much as blink at him.

"You teach gym at Lakefield Middle and have been the wrestling coach here for seven years. You've taken them to regionals three years running, which is very impressive for a school of this size. You never returned your last rental to Blockbuster before they went out of business five years ago. Your bank account has seven hundred and twenty-three dollars in it and you have lined up an under-the-table summer job at a construction firm laying concrete forms."

Alice wasn't the sort to stare. Glare maybe, if a student needed to be intimidated, but staring was for women who were easily shocked, or let themselves be surprised.

She was staring now.

"Interesting, that your last visit to Shifting Sands Resort ended up being canceled due to... what was it? Chicken pox?"

Alice didn't believe for a moment that his hesitation was anything but feigned for effect.

"It's rare for adults to contract chicken pox," the strange shifter observed. "Rarer still for shifters to get it."

"You need a note from my doctor?" Alice asked mockingly. She made herself keep her casual posture, even though she and her bear were both bristling in alarm.

"I already have it," the man said casually. "But it's a little odd that it was from a doctor in Portland. And that your airline tickets were changed at the last minute to Oregon, rather than Costa Rica. Took a bit of a hit on that, didn't you?"

Alice was done pretending. "What do you want?" she asked outright, sitting forward and planting her feet.

The stranger smiled slowly. "I have a matter of interest at the resort, a problem that has proved unexpectedly challenging."

Alice immediately distrusted his tone. "What *kind* of interest?" she demanded. "And what does this have to do with me?"

"I have an offer for you," the man said smoothly, not answering any of her questions. "One that will more than cover your time and any inconvenience. One that will more than cover the medical costs your brother needs."

Alice felt her heart drop out of her chest. "What do you know about that?" she asked fiercely, not even trying to pretend ignorance.

"I know that a million dollars will go a long way towards his care and comfort. With plenty left over to buy your parents a lovely retirement home."

Alice forced herself to act like she wasn't intimidated, though her stomach and her heart seemed to be having a wrestling match in her belly. "Oh, a million dollars," she said mockingly. "Is that all?"

"Very well," the shifter across the desk said, his mouth curving up in a smile that indicated he knew she was bluffing. "*Fifty* million. Money is no object to me."

Alice had always thought that breaking into a sweat from anything but exertion was just literary nonsense, but she did now. "Fifty million?" she murmured, in a very un-Alice way. "What exactly do you want me to do?"

He laughed, and it was a surprisingly warm laugh. "Don't look so shocked, Alice. I'm not going to have you *murder* anyone."

That had been the only thing Alice could imagine for that kind of money, but she somehow didn't feel relieved. "What is it you want me to do?" she repeated.

"The owner of the resort is a woman named Scarlet Stanson."

*You don't have to murder her*, Alice had to remind herself.

The man slid a business card across the desk. "All you have to do is find out what kind of shifter she is."

# Chapter 2

"CONALL SAYS GIZELLE'S been in her animal form for nearly the whole day, the poor dear," Laura said, sidling up beside Graham Long at the open door of the refrigerator. The wolf shifter wasn't talking to him, but to her identical twin sister Jenny, the otter shifter sitting at the kitchen bar.

"She's a little shaken by the idea of Neal coming back to Shifting Sands," Jenny explained. "He's the one who coaxed her back to human form and she was pretty broken up when he left with Mary."

"Was she in love with him?" Laura asked, slipping under Graham's arm to take a plate of leftover Alaska salmon filet and a bottle of orange juice.

"Nothing like that," Tex, Laura's bear shifter mate, was quick to assure her. "But he was the first one she really trusted. I think she's worried that Neal won't like who she is now. She's changed so much since they last saw each other."

Laura, having poured them all glasses of orange juice, ducked back under Graham's arm to return the bottle.

Graham was still standing in front of the open fridge, eyeing the contents without interest. Nothing looked appealing, but he still felt oddly hungry and his lion was pacing restlessly in his head. Finally, he snagged two cold breakfast sausages and a croissant and took a cluster of apple bananas from the fruit bowl.

The others nodded at him as Graham took the stool at the end of the bar where Laura had left him a glass of cold juice and he nodded back. That was as much conversation as they generally expected from him.

"I'm sure Gizelle will be fine once he's here and they've had a chance to reconnect," Tex said. "I'm more worried about how Conall is going to react to Neal."

Conall, Gizelle's mate, was a deaf Irish elk shifter. Losing his hearing had been devastating to his soaring music career and he had been unfriendly and prickly when he first arrived at Shifting Sands.

Gizelle's love had mellowed him considerably, and her touch allowed him to hear, but he was still cool and grim around strangers, and he was intensely protective of his mate.

Maned red wolf shifter Neal, once a prisoner in the same shifter zoo that Gizelle had grown up in, had been a hardened Marine before his capture. He had been key in helping Gizelle find her way back to her human form when they were freed, but he was not overly friendly or easy to get to know.

Now, after more than a year, he was returning to wed his mate, Mary, and would see the young woman that Gizelle had blossomed into for the first time.

"Even if Conall and Neal can't stand each other, *this* wedding should still go much more smoothly than our last one," Laura laughed. They were still picking up the pieces of the last wedding that Shifting Sands had hosted, one that had ended in a bloody duel, a happily jilted groom, and the establishment of a small shifter retirement home on the island.

"Well, Neal probably won't sue the resort, at least," Tex agreed. "And Mary isn't going to leave him at the altar to marry a waiter like Darla did. Probably."

They all laughed, except Graham, who caught his face before it could smile.

Jenny, who worked as Scarlet's lawyer, grimaced as the laughter faded.

Her mate Travis, the resort handyman, caught her expression and asked, "Any word from Darla's dreadful mother on that lawsuit she threatened?"

"Not yet," Jenny said. "But we're expecting the worst."

"Horray," Laura said humorlessly.

Jenny frowned. "What I really don't understand is why Scarlet isn't trying harder to find Aaric Lyons' heir. My firm found some really promising leads, but she's actually told me to *stop* pursuing them."

Graham hunched over his food, feeling his ears heat.

Benedict Beehag, the heir to the shifter zoo that Gizelle and Neal had been trapped in, owned the entire island and had been trying to sell it out from underneath Scarlet and dissolve their contract since he had inherited. The unfortunate part was that he seemed to be going out of his way to market it to the very worst kind of underworld characters and he had even tried to hire away Scarlet's most trusted staff in a hostile takeover.

Scarlet, with the help of Jenny, had been able to thwart his efforts at every turn, but Beehag had proved unpleasant as a landlord and had not given up trying to sell the property, though each prospective buyer seemed more unsavory than the last.

Jenny had recently discovered an obscure clause in the lengthy contract that required Beehag to give the heir of the original owner, Rupert Beehag's partner Aaric Lyons, first right of refusal on any subsequent sales of the property. Everyone had assumed the line had died out, but Jenny uncovered records for a grandson, Grant Lyons, who had moved to America and presumably changed his name.

"Money?" Laura suggested. "Even if Darla's mother *doesn't* sue, there's no way she's paying off the remainder of her bill for that wedding, and Scarlet went all out on the expenses for it. The resort can't be doing well, financially. Maybe she figures she doesn't have the funds to buy the resort, so why bother? Maybe she doesn't want to risk the funds on hiring detectives?"

Jenny shook her head. "This would be calling in favors from people I've worked for; it wouldn't even cost her. And there's a possibility—even if it's slim—that when we find him, we'll find that *Lyons'* got the money for the sale. He can't be a more unappealing landlord than our current one."

"Do you have any idea why she's balking?" Tex asked Travis. "You've been here longer than anyone but Graham."

Travis shook his head.

Graham had been studiously peeling his apple bananas, keeping his head down and hoping he didn't look guilty, and he was startled into looking up at the sound of his name.

His *fake* name.

"Do *you* have any ideas?" Laura had been looking his way and Graham scowled to cover his confusion.

He only grunted and shrugged one shoulder in answer. He was relieved when no one seemed to expect anything else.

They turned the conversation to happier plans for the upcoming wedding.

He finished his breakfast as quickly as he could, cursing the tiny, challenging peels of the miniature bananas and his own instinct to crush them rather than disrobe them.

Then he escaped, dumping his peels in the trash and leaving his plate in the sink.

He scowled to himself as he stalked to the kitchen to get Chef's request for produce from the garden.

He'd gotten used to being Graham. He *felt* like Graham.

*Graham* was someone who had friends, however reluctantly. Friends who trusted him, included him in their jokes, and even asked him for favors. Friends he actually wanted to do favors *for*.

*Graham* was hard working and quiet. He was dependable and steady. He was solid.

*Graham* was a good guy.

But he wasn't really Graham.

And Grant Lyons wasn't any of those things.

# Chapter 3

"WOULDN'T IT BE HILARIOUS if you met your mate here, too?"

Alice pretended to laugh. "Har har," she offered, hoping it sounded less bitter to them than it did to her.

Her co-worker and best friend Mary meant well, of course. And Amber, who was snickering as she climbed out of the poorly-sprung resort van, didn't have a mean bone in her body. (She also looked almost exactly like she had when she and Alice were rooming together, which was terribly unfair.) Neither of them realized how much the idea of *mates* hurt Alice.

"Oh my gosh, the entrance looks exactly the same as it did," Amber exclaimed. "Wow, the memories! The smells! The flowers! Oh my gosh, the flowers on that hyacinth!"

Mary had her nose in the air as well. "What amazing surprise has Chef concocted?" she wondered out loud.

"Pot roast," Amber deduced. "With a garlicky marinade and a side of fresh roasted radishes and some kind of onion soup, and I think chocolate for dessert."

Alice stared at her as her own bear confirmed every one of those smells in turn. "Pregnancy nose is so weird," she said in awe. "You couldn't even smell the difference between dish soap and toilet cleaner when we were rooming together."

Amber, who was not quite to the stage of waddling, but well past the dangerous-to-ask 'plump or pregnant?' phase, smiled. "It's not entirely a blessing! I had to kick the cat off the bed because she smelled like cat spit," she confided. "And if I weren't already banned from scooping the catbox, I would be incapable of it for the stench."

She reached for her bag, but Tony, coming around from the other side of the van where he'd been talking with a man he had greeted as Travis, stopped her. "You aren't supposed to carry heavy things!" he insisted, grabbing it first.

"It's not heavy," Amber protested.

Tony gave a harrumph of disbelief and shouldered the bag anyway.

"You know, women have been giving birth and carrying their own luggage for thousands of years," Amber reminded him.

"Be glad I'm not insisting on carrying *you*," Tony said, ignored the laughing protests of Travis as he scooped up half of their luggage and sailed into the resort entrance. "I know where our cottages are, you girls check in!"

Neal, Mary's mate, grinned and silently took another load of luggage in his wake.

There were other guests already queued to check in at the desk in the glorious little courtyard and while Amber and Mary chattered about weddings and babies, Alice found herself scrutinizing the woman behind the desk.

Her movements were brisk and efficient as she handed out keys and ran credit cards and shuffled forms, and Alice guessed even before she heard her introduce herself that this must be Scarlet. The brilliant red color of her hair suggested the origin of her name, though Alice kept second guessing whether or not it was dyed. It looked too bright to be natural, but too natural to be from a bottle.

Maybe the spa was *really* exceptional.

She wondered wistfully if they could do anything for her own limp, short, brown hair, then dismissed the thought. Even if they could, they couldn't do anything about the towering height or the linebacker physique, and even less about the aggressive forward nature and short temper. She wasn't the pretty, pleasing type like Amber and Mary. And she certainly wasn't here to snag a mate to marry.

It was their turn at the desk.

"Welcome back, and congratulations!" Scarlet greeted their party with a warm smile. "Please consider yourself at home and let me know if you need anything while you're here."

Though Alice thought Scarlet probably said something like that to everyone who came through, it felt particularly sincere and even grateful. Her smile included Alice, who felt uncomfortable, remembering the business card that was burning a hole in her pocket.

*At least you don't have to kill her*, she reminded herself.

Which was good, because Alice was pretty sure she wouldn't be able to do that. Not even for fifty million dollars.

Forms were spread out over the counter. "Please inspect these for accuracy, initial here and here, and sign on the last page. You received copies of the rules and requirements, but I do want to remind you that our foremost rule is no predation."

She was looking at Alice when she said that, which made sense, as the newcomer, and a scary bear shifter, but Alice wondered if there was more significance to Scarlet's glance than that.

Alice met her gaze without wavering, trying to guess her shifter type just from her characteristics; she'd been able to tell Mary was a deer shifter the first day they'd met as new teachers in middle school, and she knew that Amber was a cat shifter immediately from her feline grace, even if she never in a hundred years would have guessed Andean mountain cat, an obscure wild cat like a tiny snow leopard.

The sense of power around Scarlet was without question, but for some reason, she didn't feel like any of the large predators that Alice could think of. Something mythical? There was supposed to be a dragon lifeguard, which opened up a whole box of 'I didn't know they were real' possibilities. A gryphon? A unicorn? An... angel?

Scarlet was still looking at her, and Alice finally decided that a direct approach was a good as any.

"So, what's *your* shift form?" she asked casually.

Mary and Amber both went still beside her and she could feel their surprise without turning to look at them.

Alice grinned. "I mean, you've got all our information," she said casually, indicating the form as she scrawled her initials boldly and flipped the page over. "It's a fair question."

Scarlet only smiled coldly and kept her secrets.

"The restaurant is open for breakfast and dinner only, but the buffet is available around the clock." She pushed brochures over the counter. "The bar and spa hours are listed here, as well as yoga sessions, meditation, and dance lessons."

Oh well. Alice would have been surprised if it had been that easy.

# Chapter 4

GRAHAM ARRIVED AT THE kitchens still scowling, but no one was surprised by that.

"Morning, Grumpy," Breck called to him as he waltzed past with a tray of fruit cups. "Chef's got the list on the fridge. Let him know what you've got so we can put the rest in on the mainland order. Travis is leaving in an hour."

The resort produce garden was not all that large; it couldn't possibly provide all of the vegetables the kitchens used. But it could add a little splash of incredibly fresh produce when called upon and Graham's tomatoes were generally accepted as ambrosia from heaven.

Graham frowned over the list hung on the gleaming fridge with a heart-shaped magnet.

"Morning, Graham," Breck's mate Darla said shyly at his elbow. The snow leopard shifter was the newest addition to Chef's kitchen and still seemed timid around Graham.

Grant would have liked frightening her. Graham tried to scowl a little less and nodded in greeting.

He stepped aside to let her open the fridge and pull out a gallon jar of milk, then vanish back down one of the shining kitchen aisles to where she was mixing some mysterious dough; her failed baking lessons were commonly available in The Den, the manor where most of the senior staff lived. Most of them were perfectly edible, if too ugly for guest consumption.

Chef's progress through the noisy kitchen was made obvious by the opera he was singing at the top of his considerable lungs. "Ah, Graham," he greeted in his booming voice. "I'm not sure about the status of your tomato crop, but if you could perform a miracle and have four dozen of about this size, you would be the answer to a prayer."

Graham frowned at the example tomato Chef was holding. "I'll have to check," he hedged. Truth was he knew off the top of his head that he only had about half of that ripe now, but he might be able to cheat a little.

"And basil," Chef said, looking at the list.

"Got plenty."

"Any hot peppers ripe?"

"Few handfuls of jalapeños, a couple of chocolate habaneros." Graham had been eyeing the ripening habaneros avidly; it was a strain he'd never grown before and the plants had been reluctant to bloom in the tropical heat.

"Perfect! I'll take any you'll part with. I've got a spicy Moroccan dish that is perfect to try out on our current crowd."

Chef wandered back to check on a simmering pot and correct Darla's kneading technique. The two of them did a lilting duet from a show tune together.

Graham tucked the list into his pocket and left out the back door.

The resort was steep and non-shifters would have found the terrain challenging, but Graham climbed the steps two at a time, head down, shoulders rolled forward, face scowling, so no one would be tempted to talk to him or ask for directions.

The last of the guests from the latest flight were checking in, two of them familiar, while the third was a stranger. The two figures he recognized would be the mates of Neal and Tony, who had both been key in bringing down the shifter zoo on the opposite side of the island.

But it was the third one who caught his attention.

She was an amazon, towering over the two slighter women with her, and she had short, dark brown hair in a practical bob. She stood at easy attention, with a fit, powerful body not the slightest bit masked by her simple t-shirt and jeans. She had the barest swell of hips from behind, and a small, firm ass.

Graham forgot about talking to Scarlet, forgot about tomatoes and secret identities.

His world had narrowed to this woman and his lion was growling at his ear, intent and focused.

He could not have said how long he stood and stared as the strange woman finished signing her forms and turned at last.

Hazel-green eyes met his and every breathless suspicion was confirmed: this *was* his mate.

Others on the staff sometimes talked about how it felt to meet their mate and how they fought their instincts when they met for various reasons.

Graham was a fighter. Down at the very bones of whatever name he wore, he was a fighter, and he felt now like he did when he was preparing for battle: calm and ready and focused.

But it wasn't his instincts he was ready to fight. He crossed to the middle of the courtyard in just a few steps and she met him there.

For a long moment they stood, silently sizing each other up.

Then she growled at him, and he was lost.

# Chapter 5

ALICE APPRECIATED THE need for rules. Without rules, there were no games. Without games, there was no competition. Without competition, there was no growth.

But she still resented being read rules like she was some kind of errant kid who didn't understand that she shouldn't eat other guests.

Scarlet must have had a lawyer go over her agreement; every i was dotted and every t was crossed. And Scarlet herself... Alice knew it was too much to hope that the woman would prove to be friendly and forthcoming, but she hadn't expected the sharp, judgmental scrutiny that she got, or the intimidating power that the woman exuded.

Fifty million dollars, she reminded herself. Fifty million dollars to snoop out just one tiny detail. So Alice was so forward and friendly that she feared she was being flirtatious, asking about the resort and Scarlet's role until she was aware of Mary giving her suspicious sideways looks.

Scarlet seemed nothing but cool and professional in reply, her veneer unbroken until a leggy, cream-colored young cat leapt up onto the counter between them.

"This is Tyrant," Scarlet introduced with a tolerant smile that cracked her cool facade, scooping the kitten off the paperwork. "She doesn't understand boundaries."

Alice wondered if that was a dig at her for being nosy, but Scarlet let the three women coo over the affectionate feline and trade chin scratches for purrs, explaining that this was a real cat, not a shifter. "Though Gizelle does seem to hold out hope," she chuckled, releasing Tyrant back to the floor with a swift stroke from ears to tailtip.

Mary laughed knowingly and Amber said, "I'm looking forward to meeting Gizelle in human form at last."

Alice had heard all the stories about the shifter zoo and Gizelle's captivity. "I'm looking forward to meeting her, too," she said more boisterously than she intended.

That earned her an actual frown from Scarlet and Alice remembered that Gizelle was shy and afraid of more than Mary was. She grinned winningly back at Scarlet. Sometimes the timid students surprised her by responding well to a little encouragement. One of her best wrestling kids had been soft-spoken and terrified before joining the team.

Scarlet only looked at her more dubiously, and handed them each a key. "Let me know if you have any questions or problems," she said dismissively.

*Fifty million dollars*, Alice reminded herself, taking hers.

Then she turned away to go with Mary and Amber to their cottages... and even fifty million dollars was nothing.

He was standing at the entrance to the resort, wearing a green polo shirt with the Shifting Sands logo and khaki pants like the rest of the staff. His big hands were in fists at his side and his thick blond hair was wild around his face. He had a jaw like a brick and blue eyes like holes to the sky, and a dozen other romantic notions that meant absolutely nothing as he started to stride towards her.

Alice was in motion before she was aware of giving her feet the command, her bear roaring urgently to her as she crossed the distance to her mate.

Damn Mary for being prophetic, Alice thought fiercely. And damn her for feeling like she had a net of butterflies instead of a stomach, for the weakness and need that was burning inside her. She didn't want to swoon at his feet, and at the same time, she desperately did. It made her teeth clench, the way she wanted to give herself to him. She belonged to no one.

They were standing in the middle of the courtyard, staring at each other, and Alice was distantly aware of the surprised scrutiny of her friends, and of Scarlet.

But mostly she was aware of his strength and the height of him—he had an inch or two on her—the smell of him, and her own rising desire.

Without considering, she peeled her lips back, and growled at him wordlessly in challenge.

*What are you going to do*? she taunted him with her eyes, half-hoping he would run and prove all her fears right.

He didn't run.

He reached over and put one hand at the back of her neck and pulled her in for a bruising kiss. It wasn't a kiss that asked permission, and it wasn't a kiss that pretended to be gentle or courtly, and at some point Alice realized that she was the one kissing *him*, her arms around his broad shoulders and her mouth fierce against his.

The sound of a throat clearing made her stop at last, her mouth throbbing, and draw back.

Mary and Amber must be staring, and probably Scarlet was too, but Alice had no interest in looking away from the strange, gorgeous man's intense gaze to find out.

She wanted to ask who he was, find out why he looked so grim, hear the sound of the voice that must come from those lips, from that chest.

She wanted to know where he came from, what he'd been like as a child, what he was afraid of, what he did for fun, where those big hands had been that made them smell like dirt and grass.

She wanted to know why *him*, why *her*, what *now*...

But most of all, she needed to know, "*Where?*"

His smile was so slow, so hopeful, so utterly beautiful that it gave Alice a little unwelcome jolt in the center of her chest.

Then he was taking her hand and she was following him out of the courtyard as Mary and Amber fell into delighted laughter behind them.

# Chapter 6

THE TOUCH OF HER HAND in his was electric and Graham had to struggle to remember which of the cottages would be empty now... fourteen had just been vacated, but wouldn't be made up yet... eleven wouldn't be occupied for another few days.

And it was close, which was his primary concern now.

She smelled like a long day of travel and, beneath that, like simple soap and sunshine. Her hand was strong in his, long-fingered and rough-finished.

They made it to the intersection to the first tier of cottages before Graham had to kiss her again, to taste those wild lips and feel those hands around his shoulders.

It was with great difficulty that he managed to draw away again and get them both down the white gravel path to a cottage he hoped would be empty.

He nearly broke the door, wrenching it open, and was grateful to see that there was no luggage or personal affects within. He didn't pause in his beeline to the bed in the room beyond, and then they were wrestling down together.

She was so *strong*.

It was nearly a battle, each testing the other's strength, pushing for dominance, growling, stripping off clothing without care for seams or stitches.

This was no fainting daisy, there was no place for shyness; she knew what she wanted, what they both wanted, and she would take it if he didn't give it.

And oh, he wanted to give it to her.

As Graham kicked off his pants, she drew her nails along the length of his cock. He drew in his breath with a hiss, then pressed her down into the bed.

For a moment, she struggled with him, trying to tip him over on his back instead, and for that moment, Graham actually thought she might win the contest. Then she gave a little sigh of surrender and need and spread her legs and he was driving into her at last.

She was so wet and ready that he buried himself into her in one clean stroke and they held there a heartbeat before erupting into a frenzy of clawing and growling and thrusting.

It was like fencing, or dancing—advance, retreat, test boundaries, withdraw—and then there was a delicious moment of surrender when the woman in his arms gave a helpless noise of pleasure and went limp in his arms, giving herself completely to the release that washed over her.

That, even more than her lush, fierce, scrambling need, broke something in Graham... and he was helplessly coming with her, utterly lost to her heat and the soft, sweet noises she was making.

They lay apart at last, gasping for breath and desperate for the kiss of cool air on sweaty skin.

His mate.

He'd met his mate, and she was *perfect*.

She was strong and beautiful and fearless and there was a secret vulnerability to her that made Graham want to wrap her up in his arms and hold her safe forever.

"So, I'm Alice," she gasped in introduction, when she finally had breath for it. "Hi."

For a moment, Graham could only revel in the beauty of the name. Then he realized he needed to give his own in return and froze in indecision. Did he continue the lie he was living or start with the truth and go into the lengthy explanation his real name would require? Was he Graham, or was he Grant? Who did he want to be for his *mate*?

The window for answering politely was stretched and growing uncomfortable, and Graham felt panic rise in his throat. He needed to be cool, he needed to keep things under control. He needed to come up with something to say before she thought he was some kind of moron who didn't have a grasp of basic social skills.

"I love you," he blurted.

# Chapter 7

ALICE LAY IN A HAZE of comfortable bliss, her whole body feeling deeply satisfied.

Whoever this man was, he knew his way around her parts like he had a map, and he was strong and forward and *beautiful*.

She knew that a mate wasn't going to be the same happy ever after for her that Amber and Mary had found, but it was wonderful to revel in the sated animal need for a moment. She had the impression from her bear of rolling in sunlit flowers and having every itchy place scratched.

She supposed she should introduce herself and did, once she had breath. "So, I'm Alice," she said, staring up at the cottage rafters. "Hi."

"I love you," he replied after a moment, and Alice felt all of her contentment vanish at his words.

"Nope," Alice said firmly. "Nope, nope, nope." She sat up and supposed she should find her clothing, but whatever scraps of dignity she'd started with had been left in Scarlet's courtyard anyway.

"Look," she said, trying to find a tone that was firm but still kind, because whatever else she wanted to do, it made her chest squeeze to think of hurting him. But she couldn't string him along, either.

That would only be worse.

And she had her own life, her own troubles. She wasn't going to drag him back to that and she wasn't going to run away from what she had—her family, a job she loved—to pursue a *relationship*. She couldn't see a way that would end in anything but resentment.

"This was... great," she said. "And I know that Amber and Mary found something amazing with their mates, and that's awesome for them, but this is just sex and animal instinct, it's not destiny or nonsense like that. There's this romantic notion about mates, but it's just leftover evolutionary crap or something, it's not... fate."

He was sitting up on one elbow now, his whole face scrunched up in a glower.

Alice found his chest incredibly distracting and had to look somewhere else in order to continue forming complete sentences.

His thick arms were just as bad, and his hard jaw, and his tousled mane of hair.

He was a minefield of places she didn't dare look.

And he wasn't helping the conversation much, scowling at her like she was babbling nonsense.

Which she might have been doing, since she caught herself staring at his word-gobbling chest again.

"You don't love me," she insisted, wrenching her eyes away again. "I'm a gym teacher from the Midwest and I love my job, and you work at a fancy island resort in the tropics, and you've said three whole words to me, and none of them were your name."

"I'm Gra—Graham," he said, reluctantly.

His rumbling growl of a voice did nothing to still Alice's jangling nerves.

"Alice," she repeated and she thrust out a hand as if a formal handshake could possibly undo the sweaty, desperate sex they'd just had. "I'm glad to meet you. I am. But that's out of the way now, so don't expect a wedding date or anything, okay? We should be *honest* about this."

He continued to gaze at her, a piercing look that Alice was sure saw right through her attempt to keep him at arm's length. Whatever she said out loud, her sated body still hummed for him and her bear was still insisting that this was theirs, *forever*.

But her body was *wrong*, her bear was just an *animal* at the end of the day, and Alice was where she belonged, back in control of things.

When Graham reluctantly shook her hand, she feared she'd made another mistake, because the feel of his fingers against her palm sent shudders down her spine and made her bear... purr.

*Bears don't purr*, she told her animal crossly.

*Neither do lions*, her bear said smugly.

But clearly, until she'd shattered the moment with her declaration of nope, Graham, and the lion who obviously shared his body, had been deep in purr territory.

He wasn't now, of course, still scowling at her darkly like he was trying to figure out a puzzle.

Alice hastily reclaimed her hand.

"Oh look, there's my jeans. I'll just... ah... get dressed and go see if I can catch up with Mary and Amber." Alice crawled gracelessly off the bed, wondering how he had ever made her feel like her cumbersome body was something to be worshiped.

She tugged her pants up with effort, nearly unbalanced, and finally managed to wrench them on.

"Alice," he started, and it made the hairs at the back of her neck lift.

"Thank you," she said brightly. "This was great fun. Maybe we'll hook up again later, if I've got time. Wedding stuff, you know. Not mine. Mary's. Mary's wedding."

Her shirt was in a heap on the floor and her bra was nowhere in sight. Well, she wasn't so amply endowed that it mattered much.

She pulled the shirt over her head, discovered it was backwards, and stuffed her arms through anyway. "*Ciao!*" she called, as merrily as she could, then she was fleeing in a random direction out of the door.

# Chapter 8

GRAHAM FELT LIKE THE sun had gone out with Alice's flight, though the room was still infused with golden light through the filmy curtains. Part of him wanted to roll on the rumpled bedcovers and inhale her scent on the pillows.

The rest of him wanted to hit something.

*This is not fate.*

His lion wanted to pursue her, of course, but Graham tamped down that with a growl of his own. *Ciao* indeed. If she wanted to keep this casual, *fine*.

He was glad he hadn't told her his real name, even while he felt like he was a bottle under unbearable pressure, desperate to tell someone, anyone, especially her, who he really was, and beg for forgiveness.

One of the pillows tore apart under his hands before he could stop himself and Graham rose with a snarl to take a shower and wash her from his skin.

Her key found the bottom of his foot and he growled in pain before he picked it up and was sorry he looked at the cottage number because now he'd know where she was staying. Dammit. He put the key on the bedside table, vowing to return it to the lost and found, and stomped to the shower.

He left the cottage in utter disarray, knowing that he'd hear about it later and not caring.

Still damp, still stung, he threw himself at his garden until afternoon, tying up the bean vines that were unfurling wildly across the beds, gently thinning the new lettuce, turning fresh dirt to plant a new batch of cucumbers.

By the time the staff meeting came around, he had buried everything again and felt the familiar layer of indifference settle around him. As long as he didn't *think* about her, he wasn't angry.

And Graham was *good* at not thinking about things.

He was still carefully not thinking about anything when he arrived early at the staff meeting and he was sorry that he wasn't in a better mood, because Neal and Tony were there, grinning and catching up on all the gossip and adventure that had happened at Shifting Sands since they'd been there.

"... Which is when the boat blew sky-high and Laura and I were left adrift in the middle of the ocean," Tex was explaining.

"The fireworks were nice," Laura said, laughing. "And he sang to me!"

"Sounds romantic," Neal said with a grin.

Neal hadn't done much grinning before Mary, Graham observed, and he scowled harder than ever. Wasn't that how mates were supposed to work? His own experience was proving vastly different.

Tex went on to talk about the otter who saved them.

"That was me," Jenny explained. "Not dead after all!"

That was when Neal realized that Graham was there and he interrupted the story to rise and shake hands with a smile.

Graham shook the offered hand, but gave no reply to Neal's cheerful greeting, wondering if there were layers of meaning in his knowing grin. Would Mary have already had a chance to tell him about his unorthodox introduction to her bridesmaid?

Fortunately, Breck arrived just then and Neal turned his greeting to him, letting Graham edge into the room and find an out of the way chair to sit on. "I hear you got married? Can this be? Is it *possible*? Did she drag you kicking and screaming?"

"There was screaming and a lot of clawing," Breck conceded. "But not so much of the dragging." He was grinning broadly, his eyes soft the way they always were when he spoke of Darla. "Wait until you meet her," he added adoringly. "She's so amazing."

Graham caught himself before he could growl out loud.

Lydia came in then and gave Neal and Tony each a warm, affectionate hug, Wrench glaring over her shoulder at the strangers protectively. "You've done so much for us," she told Tony appreciatively.

"Oh, it's not so much," Tony said, abashed. "Just doing my job."

Lydia wasn't the only one who made a skeptical noise. As an agent in the Shifter Affairs department, Tony had been instrumental in getting all the shifters who had been rescued from the zoo the paperwork and legal documents to return to their lives after a period of long absence and, in many cases, presumed death. Following that, he had been extremely useful in stopping a mob boss that had been hounding Jenny, Laura, and Wrench.

Congratulations were still being exchanged, for Neal's upcoming nuptials and Tony's impending fatherhood, when Scarlet arrived to start the meeting at one o'clock on the dot.

Graham stared fixedly at the floor, refusing to look at her.

The meeting was lighthearted, centering around the details of the upcoming wedding and the day-to-day considerations of the resort. The lawsuit from Darla's mother had not materialized and, if money was tight, it appeared that they were at least fairly well set to meet the coming weeks. Scarlet was glad to report that they were going to have a steady stream of guests; the debacle of Darla's wedding had not only *not* hurt their guest list, the publicity seemed to have been largely in the resort's favor.

As Scarlet concluded the meeting and left, nearly everyone else remained and the conversation dissolved into further gossip and talk about the wedding.

"How long are you staying?" Lydia asked.

"Three glorious weeks," Amber said in delight. "The wedding is the end of next week, and we'll have a week afterwards."

"We'll be leaving the same time," Tony added. "This is our last chance for a vacation before the baby comes."

That led to excited speculation about the baby, its gender, and what its shift form might be.

Laura shyly confessed her own pregnancy news to Tony and Neal. "We haven't told Scarlet yet," she said, her hand in a beaming Tex's. "We're... not really sure what our plans are next."

Graham squirmed and looked for a way to leave that wouldn't be obvious; choosing a chair in the corner had kept him out of the conversation, but it had also trapped him in the back of the room with no polite way of slinking out.

Babies, weddings, mates, and *secrets*.

He was in hell.

Then Neal turned around in his chair to look directly at Graham and said pointedly, "Speaking of honeymoons..."

And everyone looked at him curiously.

"I hear you and Alice didn't waste any time," Neal ribbed.

Graham had liked Neal much better when he said much less.

"Alice?" Breck said, puzzled. "Mary's friend? The maid of honor?"

"Honeymoon?" Laura said curiously.

There was a moment of silence, Graham wishing he could actually make someone burst into flames with a glare.

Then Neal, oblivious to his efforts at directed spontaneous combustion, laughed. "Mary says you looked like someone had slapped you with a fish. And apparently the kiss was enough to sizzle the plants in the courtyard."

The staff erupted into congratulations and speculation.

"The last bachelor tumbles!" Travis crowed.

"I'm so happy for you," Lydia said warmly.

Wrench was sitting close enough to Graham to give him an approving punch in the shoulder and Graham turned on him with a growl.

Now that the attention was on him anyway, there was no point in trying to get out quietly. He stood and shoved through Wrench and Lydia, then plowed through the room, chairs crashing aside to a chorus of surprise.

He slammed the door so hard behind him that it rattled the artwork on the walls outside and stalked away to find something to drink.

# Chapter 9

ALICE REEKED OF SEX to her own over-sensitive nose.

Sex and strength and sun-warmed dirt and some kind of plant she didn't know.

Part of her wanted to savor it, simply revel in the heady flavor of it and enjoy the hum of satisfaction her body still clung to.

But it also made her remember his words, *I love you*, and the way her heart had responded to them.

She turned the wrong way out of the cottage when she fled and ended up dead-ending at another cottage where a pair of mountain lions were sunning on a little porch.

"Sorry, wrong turn!" She waved apologetically and turned around to creep back past the cottage she and Graham had just defiled, crossing her fingers that he wouldn't appear in the doorway.

Then she was wandering down white gravel paths at random, not sure what cottage she was in; the key that Scarlet had given her was apparently wherever her bra had gone.

Downhill took her to the beach and Alice spent an hour or more walking the length of it back and forth with her shoes in her hands, trying to make sense of the thoughts tumbling through her head. Secrets. Her family. Fifty million dollars. Mates. *Love.*

It *wasn't* love.

She turned her t-shirt around the right way, but it didn't help her head.

She finally found her way back up to the bar deck overlooking the pool. The bar itself was unmanned, but there were tempting bottles of beers in a glass-doored cooler and Alice considered taking one. Probably something stronger was called for. Probably water was smarter.

Before she could decide, a voice from behind the bar startled her. "It looks like it would taste good, but it's mostly bubbles and regret."

A woman was sitting on a milk crate behind the bar, her head just below the level of the counter. Her knees were tucked up close in front of her and clutched in skinny arms. She had long, messy brown and white braids on either side of her head and her brown eyes were big in her thin face.

"That sounds about right," Alice said dryly. She opened the door and took one, pulling the cap off without a bottle opener and taking a large gulp. "You must be Gizelle."

"We've met before," Gizelle said dreamily. "You were there the day it rains blood."

Alice raised an eyebrow at her and Gizelle shook her head firmly and stood. She was taller than Alice would have guessed from her crouched form.

"I'm Gizelle," the woman agreed, lifting her chin. "You came with Neal." She didn't offer to shake hands and stayed an almost-uncomfortable distance away.

Alice nodded. "Have you run into him yet? He was eager to see you again."

A dozen conflicted expressions passed over Gizelle's face and she shook her head. "I'm trying not to run," she explained cryptically.

"How's that working for you?" Alice asked dryly, thinking of her own flight from Graham's bed.

"Dubious results," Gizelle admitted.

Something occurred to Alice. "They say you can hear other shifters' animals, is that true?"

Gizelle blinked at her. "Yes, sometimes," she said trustingly.

"What does Scarlet's animal sound like?" Alice tried to sound casual.

Gizelle considered. "It's a whisper, even when I touch her, like wind in leaves, like a far-off song I can't understand."

Alice frowned. That wasn't much to work with. "Like... birdsong?"

"Rustling feathers..." Gizelle said in sudden alarm.

For a moment, Alice thought the beer was hitting her rather harder than she was accustomed to and she wondered if the bartender stocked shifter-strength alcohol. Then she realized that the earth beneath her feet was actually moving, shaking back and forth in a gentle rumble that subsided almost as soon as she recognized it.

An earthquake. Mary had warned her that the resort had been having little flurries of minor quakes. Cluster quakes, they were called, nothing to worry about at all.

Gizelle did not seem to share that opinion.

She dropped to the ground with a shriek of terror, curling into a tiny ball and weeping.

As Alice bent to try to comfort her, alarmed by the woman's trembling, a large figure materialized from the far side of the bar and charged at her.

"Don't you touch her!" the man roared and Alice had only a moment to register the attack before he was driving into her.

Instinct and training drove her body and without thinking, Alice was twisting and lifting and using all of his own forward momentum to throw him aside. Her beer bottle went flying across the floor, but didn't break.

He was shifter strong and fast, if not a fighter, and it was only a heartbeat before he had rolled to his feet and was facing her, snarling.

Gizelle's mate, Alice realized, from his protective defense of her. What was his name? Connor?

Before Alice could explain that she wasn't harming the gazelle shifter, another figure joined the fray, and she recognized Graham at once from his scent and his broad shoulders.

He went straight for Gizelle's mate, an animal challenge rumbling from his chest as he inserted himself between Alice and her perceived threat.

Alice was moving before his fist could land, driving into him shoulder-first, so that his blow passed harmlessly through the air to one side of the other man's face.

"Would you both stop being idiots?" she roared.

Graham lowered his fists and Gizelle's mate paused, looking between the two of them, watching their mouths rather than looking at their eyes. Gizelle herself had shifted at some point and was a tiny, trembling gazelle pressed up against the bar.

"Goddamn alpha *morons*," Alice said between clenched teeth, planting her feet. "Take a moment to assess, will you? I'm not hurting Gizelle, and he's not hurting me. Even if he wanted to, I am perfectly capable of defending myself. I don't *want* your help."

She didn't want to admit how it felt, seeing Graham streak to her defense. Even as she protested it out loud, it had struck some unexpected nerve in her chest, knowing that someone would do that for her. It struck her that he *could* protect her, if she let him, and Alice wasn't sure what to do with that idea.

She only knew that it frightened her, and made something uncomfortable happen beneath her breastbone.

# Chapter 10

GRAHAM LET HIS HANDS fall to his side as Alice berated the two of them. Conall, frowning at her mouth as he lip read her tirade, relaxed. When Gizelle timidly put her muzzle into his hand, he gave a little shudder.

"I... apologize," he said formally. "She was afraid and I reacted badly." He knelt beside the gazelle, and she seamlessly shifted into her human form, arms around his neck as she sighed into the comfort of his embrace.

Graham realized he owed an apology as well, but scowling at Alice, he couldn't find the words.

She didn't want his protection.

She didn't want anything from him.

And why should she? He didn't have anything to offer her.

"S'okay," Alice told Conall, after giving Graham a return scowl. "I think the earthquake scared her."

Gizelle looked out from the shelter of Conall's arms with big, frightened eyes. "They woke it up," she said anxiously.

"Who, sweetheart?"

"The bad people without voices," Gizelle said, then she buried her face in his chest and refused to speak.

Alice looked quizzically at them, then shook her head and went to collect her beer bottle, frowning at the wasted beer. "Okay then," she said dismissively. "It was nice to meet you, I'm going to go find Mary and Amber and take a shower as soon as I've figured out what cottage I'm in."

"Twenty-two," Graham growled, grabbing a towel from behind the bar.

Alice gave him a hard look.

"You left your key," he explained shortly as he went to mop up the spilled beer.

"Did you find my bra?" Alice asked, standing in his way with her hand outstretched for the towel.

Was it a joke? Was he supposed to laugh? Graham felt like he was on the spot, and attempted a chuckle. "Huh. Huh."

It didn't sound like a chuckle, and he felt like a fool. He wasn't even sure why he was *trying*. She'd made it perfectly clear that she had no interest in anything more than sex, and he should be *glad* for that.

"You didn't happen to *bring* the key?" Alice asked him, not impressed by his terrible attempt to laugh.

Graham shrugged. He'd forgotten the key in the cottage after his shower. "It won't be locked." He gave her the towel.

"Great." Alice turned away dismissively to clean up the mess and Graham turned and left the bar rather than watch her bend over the way he desperately wanted to.

Jenny caught him as he walked into The Den, excited and bubbling over with news. "We got a lead!" she said, grinning.

Graham stared at her, not sure of the topic or an appropriate response. He was pretty sure she wasn't talking about Alice.

"Tony was able to get a little more information on Grant Lyons for us," Jenny explained in answer to his confused glare. "Most of it is in a sealed plea deal, but we found out where he did time, and why."

Graham's blood turned to ice. They knew. They *knew* what Grant Lyons had done.

"Did Scarlet change her mind about trying to find him?" Bastian asked, flipping through the mail on the counter.

Jenny shook her head, dark curls bouncing. "We're just going to keep looking quietly," she said, her eyes dancing. "Think about it! What if we could find him? What if he's still rich and could buy the island? Beehag and his asshole lawyer wouldn't be able to stop the sale and we wouldn't be wondering week to week if they were going to be able to find a way to break the resort lease just to spite Scarlet."

"What does Benedict Beehag have against Scarlet anyway?" Saina asked, reaching over Bastian to pick a fashion magazine out of the pile.

"Well, Scarlet was there when they broke up the zoo and his uncle died," Bastian suggested. "Maybe he blames her for his uncle's death?"

"I never got the idea that Allistair and Benedict were close," Jenny said thoughtfully. "I just get the feeling that Benedict doesn't like the *resort*. Maybe he's got something against shifters. I mean, his uncle did keep them in cages; maybe the whole family has some grudge against them."

Graham's limbs had thawed enough to consider creeping past for his room when Breck and Darla came laughing down the hallway, arms around each other.

"We got more information on Grant Lyons," Jenny told them, excited, and Graham stalked past, then stopped just far enough down the hallway that he could listen, heart at the bottom of his stomach, but not be seen shamelessly eavesdropping.

"Do tell!" Breck was always up for gossip and news.

"We found out why he was in prison, and where," Jenny said avidly. "Which gives us more clues about friends from his past who might know where he is."

Graham leaned against the wall, feeling the tiniest shiver of relief. They wouldn't have any luck pursuing friends. Grant Lyons didn't have *friends*.

"What did he do?" Darla asked softly. "To be put in jail, I mean?"

Any relief Graham had been reveling in vanished into despair at Jenny's words. "He killed some guy. Most of the details were obscured as part of his plea deal."

Darla made a little noise of dismay.

Graham closed his eyes against the memories that still kept him awake most nights.

"Are we sure we want a *murderer* to own the resort?" Bastian asked skeptically.

*You don't*, Graham wanted to tell him.

"It sounds like an improvement to me," Breck said. "Besides, it's not like all of us have shiny clean slates. *Graham* was in jail for manslaughter, and we trust him. Laura worked for the mob. Wrench's hands aren't particularly clean..."

Graham held his breath, waiting for them to put the pieces together.

He wanted them to, he realized. He wanted them to figure it out, so he didn't have to tell them or suffocate under the weight of the secret.

Instead, Saina changed the subject, perhaps worried that she would be next in Breck's list; she had not always been scrupulous about the use of her siren magic. "Amber's asked us to help throw a bachelorette party for Mary. Should we have it here, or at the bar?"

"Let's do it here," Jenny said eagerly. "We can kick the boys out and do daiquiris!"

"You don't have to kick *all* the boys out," Breck suggested slyly. "It's traditional to have a stripper at these affairs and I will reluctantly let you demean me in this manner."

"*Reluctantly*," Bastian scoffed, as the others laughed.

"Only if it's hands-off," Darla said possessively. "And I get to watch!"

From the giggles, Breck must have tickled or poked her. There was the sound of a kiss, murmurs about a private show, and more laughter.

The conversation flowed to the party, and the wedding, and Graham trudged on to his room, feeling ashamed and angry and aching.

He wanted to be someone different, someone better. He wanted to deserve his friends' trust. He wanted his past to stop haunting him.

Graham closed the door quietly behind him and leaned on it with a groan.

He *wanted* Alice.

# Chapter 11

DINNER WITH MARY, AMBER, and their mates was straight-up torture.

They all knew that Graham was Alice's mate, and that she had slept with him, and if they didn't know the details of their parting, they at least knew that it hadn't exactly ended with pledges of devotion.

*I love you*, he'd said.

Well, *she* hadn't ended it with pledges of devotion.

If her dinner partners didn't say anything directly, their careful choice of topics and thoughtful sideways glances sent the message quite clearly: they thought she was being crazy.

She *felt* crazy.

She felt as loony as the gazelle shifter and she desperately wished she could get away with shifting and running away to escape the awkward dinner and her own awkward self.

But being shy and eccentric as a small, delicate antelope was a lot different than it was as a giant, clumsy brown bear and Alice knew it would only be ridiculous if she tried. To say nothing of destructive.

So she plowed through the meal and the conversation with bullish cheer, praising the food, making observations about the weather, and expressing gratitude that Mary had chosen not to put the bridesmaids in heels—in part because of Amber's advancing pregnancy and in part because Alice already towered over most of the wedding party.

It occurred to her rather suddenly that Tony had been investigating Scarlet when he first came to the resort; she had been near the top of his list of suspects for the disappearing shifters that Beehag had been kidnapping. Had he figured out what her animal shift form was in that time?

It was far preferable to think about the uncomfortable topic of her real mission on the island than it was to think about Graham.

Alice steered the conversation to ask about their original visits to the island.

Mary and Neal laughed about his attempts to avoid her when they met.

"I couldn't figure it out," Mary chuckled. "I'd catch sight of him and it was like I was wearing roadkill perfume—he was suddenly fleeing in the opposite direction."

"Not my finest hour," Neal agreed, smiling fondly at her. "But sometimes, it's a rocky path to true love."

Everyone very carefully did not quite look at Alice.

"What about you, Tony?" Alice asked brightly. "You were actually here investigating Scarlet, weren't you? Did you find out any juicy secrets about her before you got distracted by meeting Amber and breaking up Beehag's zoo? Everyone's dying to know what her shift form is."

She did her best to sound casual, but the looks she got suggested she had not moved past *crazy* in their minds.

"Most of what came up in the investigation is classified," Tony said apologetically. "But no, we never did find out what she is."

Then the dessert tray was brought by Chef himself, the cook with arms like barrels and a warm, friendly smile in his handsome, graying face.

"Strawberry cheesecake," Alice selected from the tray.

"An excellent choice," Chef said, as he set the artful little plate in front of her. They were small strawberries, but a generous portion of them, deep red and drizzled with a matching sauce. "These strawberries are grown here on the island by our very own Graham and were picked this morning. He's a masterful gardener, and we're lucky to have a selection of his fresh fruit and produce."

*Of course* Graham had grown the strawberries. Alice gave the chef a suspicious sideways look, not sure if the mention of Graham was deliberate or not. Probably everyone knew about them by now. It wasn't that big an island.

It was too late to change her mind, so Alice smiled. "Sounds great!" she squeaked.

"That looks amazing!" Amber agreed with a sly sideways look. "I'll have one, too."

"I couldn't eat another bite," Mary groaned, while their mates picked out their own desserts.

"Eating for two," Amber said merrily.

Alice didn't want to start eating before they were all served, so while the others talked about pregnancy and joked about having to roll Amber to their cottage, she stared at her strawberries—strawberries that Graham had planted, nurtured... plucked with those big, strong hands...

*Damn it.*

Her bear's fire had only been dampened and now it rose again in her, swamping logical thought.

Amber's cheesecake was swiftly brought out and Alice finally took a tentative bite: creamy cake of a perfect consistency, just the right amount of sweet and deliciously cool in the hot tropical evening... and one flawless strawberry.

It was an amazing flavor combination and Alice closed her eyes and savored it, until she realized she was remembering the taste of Graham's kiss.

She ate the rest with mechanical efficiency, trying to keep up with the dinner small talk and not sound like she was thinking about a splendidly shirtless Graham feeding her strawberries.

As they gathered up to leave the restaurant at last, Amber said firmly, "You boys go on ahead! We'll catch up!"

Alice knew what they were planning and was not surprised when Amber and Mary each took an arm and steered her to the bar rather than to the paths that led to the rental cottages.

She could have shaken them off; despite being shifters, both of them together did not have the strength to make her do anything she didn't really want to. But they were her friends and she knew that if she didn't have this conversation now, it would be an even more awkward one later.

She shoved images of Graham and strawberries firmly from her head as Mary ordered drinks for all of the, and met their appraising gazes with her chin up.

"So, what's going on with you and Graham?" Amber finally asked.

Mary added, "We didn't actually expect you to join us for dinner tonight. Or to see you much at all the next few days, to be honest."

"We've got a wedding to get ready for," Alice said innocently. "I couldn't just leave you guys hanging."

Mary and Amber exchanged looks that could only be described as deeply skeptical.

"That doesn't answer the question," Mary said firmly.

Alice sighed, noisy and unladylike. "Look, I'm really happy for both of you. But that's not how mates always work out. The sex was great and that's all there was. We both have our own lives already. He doesn't fit into mine and I'm not going to give up my job to move here. You know how much I love my job! I took our team to state three years running! Anyway, a mate isn't true love or any nonsense like that."

Mary and Amber looked confused.

"You like him, don't you?" Mary asked.

"What's to like?" Alice said as carelessly as she could. "He's hot and he's built, but he's said maybe two complete sentences to me, under duress. That's not much to build a friendship on, let alone a relationship."

One of the sentences had been *I love you*, she remembered, and she was painfully grateful when the cowboy bartender brought them drinks: a fancy fruit thing with an umbrella for Mary, a virgin version of the same for Amber, and a stout glass of whiskey on the rocks for Alice.

*Real girly*, she thought with a grimace. *A catch like me, it's a wonder I'm not beating off the men.* She toasted Amber and Mary and downed half of it in a swallow.

She was rewarded with a burn down her throat that held no candle to the burning in her belly.

# Chapter 12

GRAHAM HAD FORGOTTEN all about the tomatoes Chef had requested the day before and he didn't think about them again until he received a text from Scarlet asking him to see her in her office 'at your convenience.'

*At your convenience* generally meant *drop what you're doing and get here right now*, so Graham aborted the morning workout that he'd been planning on and hiked immediately to the top of the resort, not even bothering to change into his staff uniform first.

He wondered if that gave the wrong impression when Scarlet raked him with her glance and frowned. "Should I be expecting your resignation?"

For a moment, Graham was deeply confused. Then he remembered. *Alice.*

Not that he'd forgotten her for a single moment since he had laid eyes on her—her intoxicating hazel eyes, the defiant tilt of her chin, the waves of her sensible, short hair—but he hadn't considered that Scarlet might not know that Alice didn't want him.

Oh, she had *wanted* him, had answered his desire with her own passion and heat, but she hadn't wanted *him*.

*It's not fate,* she'd said flatly. *Just leftover evolutionary crap or something.*

And who could blame her? Graham was no prize. He offered her nothing.

Graham realized he was scowling at Scarlet and hadn't answered her. "I'm not going anywhere," he growled.

Scarlet raised an eyebrow at him. "Should I be finding a position here for Alice?" she prompted. "What are her qualifications?"

Graham gave a defiant shrug. "Don't think she's interested in moving here." Hearing the words out loud was like a punch to the gut. He thought he'd made peace with it, but no part of him actually had.

Scarlet's eyes went soft, which was the last thing Graham wanted or needed. "I'm... sorry to hear that," she said gently.

Graham refused to lower his gaze, despite the discomfort hers always caused and, for once, she looked away first.

"What did you need?" he asked gruffly.

If he had not been staring at her, he would have missed the little sigh she gave and the fall to her shoulders. "I wanted to know what your plans for the future were," she said neutrally. "Because I am considering closing the resort and filing for bankruptcy, and if you were leaving that would simplify the decision."

The defiance went out of Graham in a shocked, sympathetic rush. "You... can't do that."

"I don't have a lot of choices," Scarlet snapped.

"The lawsuit," Graham guessed.

Scarlet picked up a heavy stack of paperwork and let it drop back to the desk with a thump. "The anticipated gift from the generous and benevolent Jubilee Grant."

Graham frowned. "As bad as you thought?"

"Four hundred and fifty thousand for cancellations, loss and damages. Eight hundred and twenty thousand for *mental anguish*. As a bonus, a copy of a report to the Costa Rican government that we should be investigated for food sanitation violations."

She moved that aside and picked up a manila envelope with a familiar logo on it. "As if that weren't enough, Beehag's asshole lawyer is trying to use the lawsuit as a reason to break our lease."

Graham grunted. None of this was good news. "Can you fight it? Have you shown it to Jenny?"

"I haven't told her yet," Scarlet said, with a shake of her head. "It only came in this morning, and we have some time to formulate our responses. Let everyone enjoy the wedding without this hanging over their heads. I'm sorry to burden you with it."

"It's not a—" Graham broke off with a grunt of surprise as a small form bumped against the back of his calf and gave his ankle an affectionate rub. He didn't bother to finished the sentence as the leggy, cream-colored cat walked into the room like she owned it and launched herself up onto Scarlet's desk.

"Tyrant," Scarlet greeted, as gravely as if she was a shifter and not a normal cat.

Tyrant had been a gift intended for Gizelle, but she had clearly chosen Scarlet as her primary companion, to the amusement of everyone at the resort... except Scarlet.

Tyrant gave a mrrr of greeting and tried to investigate the paperwork, reaching a paw for the shining closure on the manila envelope. Scarlet scooped her up from the desk and cuddled her in a brief, unexpected display of warmth, rubbing her cheeks and coaxing a whisker-quivering purr from the half-grown cat before setting her down on the wide window sill behind her. Several potted plants had been replaced by a cushion, and Tyrant blinked happily at the sunlight pouring in and began to groom herself, still purring.

When Scarlet turned back to Graham, her face was cool and serene again. "Please don't say anything to anyone," she said firmly, not really making it a request. "I haven't made any firm decisions yet, and there's no reason to put a pall over everything."

"I won't say anything," Graham agreed, keenly aware of the growing weight of the secrets he was keeping.

He felt Alice's presence a split-second before Scarlet frowned. "Can I help you?"

# Chapter 13

ALICE HAD A KEEN SENSE for 'interrupting something awkward.' Teaching middle school students was basically made of those moments.

The door to Scarlet's office was open and Alice was drifting in before she realized that the warm, welcoming sensation she was feeling was only from her bear, recognizing Graham's broad back before Alice even registered it.

"I won't say anything," he was growling, in that voice that made her shiver despite her best efforts.

"Can I help you?" Scarlet asked sharply.

For a moment, Alice completely forgot why she had come, her senses swamped with Graham. *Down girl*, she told her bear firmly. She smiled resolutely, ignoring the tension in the room and pretending her own entrance hadn't been its own special form of awkward. "Yes, actually!" she said cheerfully. "I'm putting together the scrapbook for Mary's wedding, and I had some questions I was hoping you could help me answer..."

Graham glanced at her once and looked away so quickly that Alice wondered if eyeballs could get whiplash.

Then he turned and walked out without a single word more, leaving her feeling irrationally bereft.

*I don't need him*, she reminded herself.

Her bear had strong alternate opinions.

She looked back to find Scarlet giving her an unreadable look and laughed inelegantly. "He doesn't say much, does he?"

Scarlet looked at her without saying anything for a long moment, then smiled rather stiffly and moved the pile of paperwork before her on the desk off to the side. "Was there something specific you were looking for?" she asked politely, gesturing to the chair opposite. "For your... scrapbook?"

Alice wondered if there was sympathy in Scarlet's eyes and decided she would take a conversation out of pity if it would help her find more clues. She sat down in the chair and made a show of opening the notebook that she had taped a few photos of Mary and Neal to.

"I was hoping you had some photographs of their visit here, or maybe some stories."

"I'm afraid I don't," Scarlet said simply.

Alice didn't really have a plan, other than to try to get Scarlet to open up and start chatting.

"Well, I was thinking about doing a bit about the resort itself, since that's where they met. Can you tell me a little about how it got started and when you took it over?"

Scarlet regarded her for a moment, and then said, with suspicious neutrality, "The resort was designed and nearly entirely built by Aaric Lyons in the early 80s. Upon his disappearance, his wife sold this half of the island to Beehag. Four years ago, I secured a lease to restart the resort and got it into operation."

"That must have been a lot of work," Alice said encouragingly.

"Yes," Scarlet answered briefly. Then, reluctantly, "I have an excellent staff."

"Graham and Travis were among the first people working here, right?" Dammit, how had the topic gotten around to Graham? Alice stumbled on. "It was almost forty years—the jungle must have really grown everything over in that time. I bet it took a long time to cut back the overgrowth."

Scarlet was silent.

"So, um, okay..." Alice looked down at her pathetic scrapbook, trying not to think about Graham with a machete, beating back jungle vines. Shirtless.

"You're not really here looking for information about Mary and Neal," Scarlet observed.

Alice blushed. She was *terrible* at this spy stuff. She thought about her brother, and her parents, and had to make an effort to draw herself together. Scarlet made her feel like she'd been called to the principal's office. Did she know about the man with the business card who had sent Alice? N. Padrikanth Moore, the pretentious name had been, no business name, or logo, or any hints as to what kind of person he was. But good people didn't generally make offers of fifty million dollars to snoop shifter types out.

"I'm sorry to pry," she said hastily. "I really was hoping to put something nice together for them, but I've kind of run into a dead end." She gave the most natural smile she could manage. "I didn't mean to be a bother."

Scarlet's expression became... complicated. It wasn't disgust and it wasn't anger, but it also wasn't quite pity, or anything else Alice could put her finger on.

"Graham," Scarlet said quietly.

Alice stared at her in consternation. If there was anything worse than Scarlet knowing that Alice was a spy, it was Scarlet thinking Alice was pining over the gorgeous gardener who had upended her life by turning out to be her mate.

Even if she sort of *was*.

Scarlet's gaze was unsettling, even when she was clearly trying to be gentle. "Graham is a good man," she said evenly. "He's quiet, but clever, and he works very hard. He is kind. He would treat you well."

This was a hundred times worse.

Alice tried to laugh and failed spectacularly. "I'm sure he is. Er, I'm sure he would. Ah, thank you," she squeaked. "I don't think it's going anywhere, though. I've got... a job, you know. He... has a job. Jobs we love. Jobs we need. Good jobs." She clamped her mouth shut, knowing she had said job entirely too many times in a row... and now she could only think about blowjobs, because her traitor bear was feeding her memories of Graham's naked splendor and she was helpless in the rush of desires that had come with talking about him at all.

If Scarlet had a clue what was going on in her head, Alice didn't want to know. "I'm really sorry I bothered you," she said desperately, rising to her feet. She knew which battles to concede. "Thank you for your time. Lovely resort. Great food."

And she fled out into the courtyard, shutting the door behind her out of habit.

She didn't get far, only as far as the bench in the courtyard, where she collapsed and tried to get her tangled mind in order.

She shoved Graham—and his glorious cock—from her mind with effort. She had to make some progress with Scarlet's shift form. She had to, or she could kiss her only hope for saving her family goodbye.

Alice drew in deep breaths, searching for her usual calm and carefree attitude. She wasn't going to get much out of Scarlet directly, she was sure. But she could use her senses.

With each breath came smells.

Usually, it was just a wild symphony of scents, all tangled together in an overwhelming disharmony that no one else seemed to notice. But if she concentrated, she could pick them out... a wolf shifter had been here... maybe Laura? No, a different wolf. Another bear, as well, perhaps Tex, but just as likely a guest.

Most shifters came through the courtyard in human shape; she could smell soap and sweat and alcohol, leather and plastic from luggage, the tang of grease from their wheels, tantalizing whiffs of the breakfast Chef must be finishing up at the restaurant, the undertone of saltwater on the breeze.

She could smell the little cream-colored cat with Siamese points in orange and its deodorizing cat litter. She could smell the paper of the mail on Scarlet's desk, the distinct musty old book smell; all of Scarlet's books appeared to be older, well-used books.

And muffling it all were the flowers and vines and potted plants throughout the courtyard. Over the vivid, pushy jungle smells, Alice couldn't pick out any animal scent that was strong enough to be someone who lived here. The strongest of the animal scents was actually lion—Graham's lion, specifically—musky and earthy and irresistible. Alice gritted her teeth and pushed to her feet.

She was getting nowhere, fast, and she could feel her chance slipping through her fingers. She realized she'd been crying as the tears started to dry on her cheeks, and scrubbed them away defiantly.

She *had* to find out what Scarlet was.

There was no other choice.

# Chapter 14

GRAHAM PEELED OFF HIS gardening gloves at the end of the row and sat back on his heels. Did she have to be so hot?

Alice was relentlessly disturbing to him, with the proud lift to her jaw and the soft mane of her short hair. Even the way she stood, alert and poised on those long, long legs... and worst of all were her hazel eyes, glittering and full of challenge.

Graham wasn't sure if he wanted to answer that challenge or simply sink to his knees at her feet in surrender the way his lion was sure they should.

He had no interest in running into Alice by accident, so even though he was hungry after a morning of work, Graham gave the buffet a wide berth and found himself sitting behind the hotel at the picnic table he had gotten in the habit of eating at with Breck and Neal before the latter had moved away from the island with his mate.

It somehow didn't surprise him when Neal appeared, carrying a tray from the buffet.

"How the tables have turned," the red-maned wolf shifter said wryly. "Sandwich?" When Neal had first come to Shifting Sands, it had been hard for him to accept Scarlet's generosity. Breck and Graham had taken to discreetly bringing extra food to share at the picnic table so he didn't have to select his own food from the buffet.

Graham shrugged, then nodded. "Thanks."

Even a second-rate sandwich from the buffet was something you didn't turn down. Scarlet insisted on the highest quality of everything; the bread was fresh and fluffy, the meat was cold and flavorful, paired with a creamy cheese, lettuce from Graham's garden, and a spicy mustard.

"I didn't mean to embarrass you in front of everyone," Neal said, after a few moments of eating in silence. "It sounded like you... hadn't wasted time."

Graham hunched miserably over his meal and didn't respond.

No, she hadn't wasted any time explaining exactly how there was nothing between them but *leftover evolutionary crap.*

"The gang's all here!" Breck's bright voice was the last thing that Graham wanted to hear, but the waiter appeared around the corner of the hotel, carrying his own tray. "Brought an extra sandwich for old time's sake," he said with relish. "But if you guys are all set, I can throw myself on that bomb."

Without waiting for an invitation, he scooted in next to Graham on the bench. "Shove those big muscles over, flower-boy."

The waiter made a production of enjoying his first bites with relish. "Scarlet may be a terrible harpy, but she lays a good spread," he said approvingly.

"She's not so much of a harpy as all that," Neal protested. "I think it's an act; she's always been bighearted by action. Even if she constantly swears she isn't running a..."

"Charity!" Breck finished with Neal. They chuckled.

Graham thought about Scarlet's dismal news and the defeat in her face that she had tried so hard to mask and could dredge up no humor, taking a vicious bite of his sandwich.

"All we need to complete this reunion is Gizelle," Breck observed. "Grazing off over there, pretending we don't exist. Have you seen her yet?"

Neal frowned and shook his head. "I figured I'd let her find me herself, so I haven't gone looking."

"You won't believe how she's bloomed," Breck said warmly. "She's usually human now, brushes her hair—or lets Conall do it—wears clothes most of the time. She helps out at the bar sometimes, hasn't broken any glasses in weeks."

"Conall, he's good for her?" Neal asked cautiously.

"So good," Breck assured him. "I thought he was a giant, angry jerk when we first met, but he loves that young woman more than anything and she adores him right back. He spoils her rotten, and fortunately she's too naive to take advantage."

"He threw a guy who was harassing her into the swimming pool," Graham added, though he had intended to stay out of the conversation.

"Oh yeah, that was a sight," Breck laughed. "A deer the size of a mammoth and this mangy, wet bully of a big-mouthed bear. Scarlet marched that jackass straight off the island, you'd better believe it."

"Good," Neal said with satisfaction. "I'm glad she's safe here."

It suddenly occurred to Graham to wonder what would happen to Gizelle if Scarlet closed the resort. As far as she'd come, as remarkable as her progression had been, she would have a hard time adjusting to a place with normal humans, and she still lacked understanding of many social norms. No one at Shifting Sands cared that she wasn't polite or didn't remember to wear clothing, but she still reacted to new things with fear and had a habit of shifting to her gazelle form and fleeing if there were loud noises.

Neal was wrong. She wasn't safe here. None of them were.

Guilt swamped Graham.

"Speaking of safe," Neal said leadingly.

"What's up with you and Alice?" Breck asked more bluntly, when Graham didn't look up.

Graham shrugged one shoulder and stuffed as much sandwich in his mouth as he could manage. "Nothing."

"What do you mean nothing?" Breck demanded. "She's your mate!"

Graham shrugged the other shoulder and knew that both of them were staring at him without having to look up.

"Was it a problem in bed?" Breck asked drolly.

Graham almost choked on his sandwich. "No!" *A hundred times no.*

"Did you... insult her?" Neal guessed.

"No," Graham said shortly. Not unless *I love you* was an insult.

Maybe it was, from someone like him.

"Did you say *anything*?" Breck asked suspiciously.

Graham shrugged.

"Did you at *least* tell her your name?" Neal demanded.

That earned them a grunt that might have been a laugh. He'd told her *a* name.

Graham still wondered if it had been the wrong name. He put the rest of the sandwich in his mouth and swallowed.

"Look," he said gruffly. "I appreciate that you're trying to help, but she's got a job. At the end of her vacation, she's going back to it. *I've* got a job, too, and I'm going back to it now."

He rose from the bench and stalked off, wondering dismally exactly how long his own job was going to last... and what he would do after that.

# Chapter 15

ALICE LAY IN HER BED, listening to the night sounds around her little cottage, wishing she could sleep.

A sheet wasn't warm enough. A blanket was too warm. The pillow was too flat, but two were too much. No position was comfortable.

And she couldn't stop thinking of Graham.

It wasn't just the sex, as mind-blowing as that had been. It was the hurt and longing in his eyes that he couldn't quite hide, it was the way he'd smiled at her when they first met, slow and full of depth. It was all the questions she wanted to ask him, all the stories she wanted to tell him.

By the time dawn's light started to creep around the curtains, she was gritty-eyed and grouchy, and tired of trying to sleep.

Alice got up and yanked her clothing on, then wandered quietly out of her cottage, up the white gravel paths towards the restaurant. Singing voices, light, and laughter spilled out of the closed doors of the kitchen, but the restaurant was as empty as she had expected for the hour of the day.

She wandered along the buffet for a moment because she felt restlessly hungry, but the food offered was no more satisfying than her bed had been. She took a piece of rolled lunch meat out of a sense of obligation and munched it as she left the restaurant.

At the door, she turned right, up the steep resort, towards the spa and the office. If she was canny, could she surprise Scarlet shifting? Maybe she was some kind of alien and Alice could catch her coming out of a cocoon...

She tripped over the corner of a potted plant at the corner of the courtyard; it didn't fall, but it rattled in the plant stand, and Alice turned and fled, cursing her uselessness as an investigator.

"You're up early," a gentle voice greeted her and she turned to find a beautiful Latina woman holding a yoga mat coming from the spa.

"Jet lag!" Alice said with false brightness. "My internal clock is all out of whack! Traveling would be so much easier without the traveling part, you know."

"I'm about to go start a sunrise yoga class," the woman said kindly. "Would you care to join me?"

"I... er..." Alice couldn't think of a good reason not to. "I don't have a mat?"

The other woman laughed. "Most guests don't. We can stop by the activity center and get one there. I'm Lydia." She offered a slight, gentle hand and Alice tried not to crush it.

"I'm Alice."

That earned her a second, thoughtful look. Alice could only imagine what she'd heard.

But Lydia didn't bring Graham up, only asked how Alice was liking her stay so far and chatted sweetly about the resort and the weather as they picked out a mat for her to use and walked past the pool to a wide lawn overlooking cliffs past the beach.

Apparently, Alice was the only one to show up for the class and she was keenly aware of her clumsy, over-sized body as Lydia, lithe and impossibly bendy, took her through a challenging series of poses.

They talked casually as they stretched and Lydia mildly corrected her posture.

"About Graham..." she finally said, exactly as Alice had been dreading.

Alice groaned, letting her head fall limp. Lydia had picked a moment when it would be challenging and graceless to storm off; she was leaning on her hands, with her butt in the air.

"Graham is a bighearted man. He doesn't have a lot to say, but he's clever and he's kind. You should give him a chance."

It was eerily similar to what Scarlet had said. Alice gave up her pose and sat down with a thump. "I'm sure he's a great guy," she said, and she was alarmed at the longing she heard in her own voice. She cleared her throat. "But I have a job back home, and he has a job here, and I just don't see a life where either one of us is willing to throw what we already have away."

Lydia looked at her thoughtfully. "Do you know a lot of mated couples?"

Alice snorted. "Not one, until Mary brought hers home."

"When I met Wrench, I knew he was for me, but... I had this idea of what he ought to be that he wasn't. I wasn't disappointed, but it took some adjustment. I had to get past his rough exterior and street speech and swearing, and once I did I found this amazing man who I needed to spend the rest of my life with. It could be the same, for you. Don't be put off by the fact that Graham was in jail, or that he can seem distant."

Was Wrench really a name? Alice wondered. Then the rest of Lydia's soft-spoken statement caught up with her.

"Graham was in jail?" Alice exclaimed. "For what?"

For the first time, Lydia looked flustered. "Oh, I'm sorry. I assumed you knew. It's not really a secret. But it's not such a bad thing. My own mate was in jail for a while. And I was alarmed when I found out, too."

"What was he in jail for?" Alice repeated. "Graham, I mean."

Lydia hesitated, then said, "Manslaughter. None of us know the details, but manslaughter is usually just an accident."

"Huh," Alice replied.

"But Graham is more than his rapsheet," Lydia was quick to say. "Just like Wrench is. And don't be put off by fact that he is so cool and reserved. He'll take patience to get through to, but he has a warm heart under that gruff exterior. It might take a long time to get him to open up, but he deserves that chance."

"Cool and reserved?" Alice scoffed. "Good god, the man declared his love for me before I found out his name."

Lydia blinked at her, but seemed to have reclaimed her calm. "Then why aren't you with him?"

"This isn't the basis for a *relationship*," Alice insisted. "I'm glad it worked out for you and... Wrench? Really? Okay... but I'm not looking for a man and I don't have room in my life for one. And Graham wouldn't be happy there anyway."

Lydia continued to gaze at her, not judgmentally, but patiently.

"I'm six foot four and turn into a bear that could eat his face off," Alice said desperately. "I live in a tiny apartment and have a high-stress job teaching ungrateful middle school students. I'm constantly traveling for sports events. I'm just... not girlfriend material."

"Graham doesn't care about that," Lydia assured her confidently. "Let's end our session in five minutes of child's pose, to lengthen our backs, open our hips, and ease our stress."

Alice obediently knelt and leaned her head forward onto the mat. She sighed into the stretch.

Graham *didn't* care about any of that, she thought achingly. She actually believed him when he said he loved her. He would go back to Minnesota with her in a hot minute, if she asked him to. He would give up his perfect life here, with his friends, doing something he enjoyed in paradise, and he would follow her to... what?

To her hardscrabble life in a snowy state with strangers? He wouldn't fit in her tiny apartment in Lakefield and she could barely afford it already. She couldn't possibly put food on their table, and as far as she knew, jobs for landscaper *felons* were not available in any abundance. She couldn't take care of Graham... she couldn't even take care of the family she *had*.

Before she could stop herself, tears leaked out of her eyes and she was glad that her forehead was down on the mat.

She was trying so hard not to think about her family, because it only made her feel helpless and despairing.

Why couldn't her mate have been a billionaire, like Gizelle's deaf musician? she wanted to wail... but the brief, ungrateful thought made her chest squeeze with guilt and regret. The sad fact was, Graham was everything she wanted in one sexy package and the more she reluctantly learned about him, the more she wanted to comfort him, to pull him into her arms and kiss him and show him that she knew who he really was beneath that quiet facade and checkered past.

Yoga, she decided, let her think too much. Once Lydia finally released her from this torture, she was going to go find the workout room that Neal and Tony had talked about and do something that would distract her more thoroughly. Maybe they had a punching bag, because she really felt like hitting something.

# Chapter 16

"YOU'LL HURT YOURSELF, hitting the bag that way," Graham had to say.

He didn't want to say anything, he wanted to slink out of the staff gym before Alice noticed him. But he couldn't let her continue to batter at the bag that way, couldn't bear to think of her in pain if he could do anything to stop it.

Alice was panting and sweaty, and the strong, gorgeous lines of her long body were fierce and graceful. "I suppose you're some kind of fighter?" she said angrily, giving the heavy bag another furious, flawed hit.

*Some* kind of fighter, Graham thought.

"You'll fracture your wrist," he growled. "Hold it straight, like this, and step back a little, so the force goes all the way up to your shoulder when you make the hit. Those are the big muscles that can take it. Wrists are weak."

He'd broken enough of them to know, he thought regretfully.

Alice gave the bag another hit, a better hit, and the bag shuddered on its chain. "Hot damn," she said, pleased. "Thanks."

Graham turned to go, but Alice stopped him with a word, "Wait..."

Graham stared at the door jamb.

"We're grownups," Alice said. "If you want to use the workout room at the same time, we... should be able to do that. If you want to lift, I can spot you. Or, whatever."

Bench presses, with her curves above him, shining with sweat? Graham wasn't that stupid.

But the only excuse he could think of to retreat from his workout involved admitting that he didn't think he'd be able to concentrate with the distraction of having her in the same room. And that sounded weak.

He grunted and went to do sit-ups on the inclined bench.

Predictably, he lost count, listening to Alice continue to punch at the bag, and then start arm curls. After he guessed he'd done a few hundred, he realized in a panic that he should probably switch, or it would look like he was incapable of doing anything else.

Pull-ups on the bars would have been his next stop, but Graham became aware that he probably should only do things that involved sitting; he was irresistibly aroused, and it was going to be obvious if he wasn't careful.

He made the mistake of glancing over at her, and she was looking away swiftly. Her color was high, but Graham told himself that might have been due to exertion. The day was hot and the fan in the workout room was not helping much.

What he really wanted to do was punch something, and the heavy bag was tempting. If he put his back to her... Graham was moving before he could reconsider, wrapping his hands with efficient motions to save his knuckles.

Crack.

The hit was always satisfying, and the chains groaned. If Travis hadn't reinforced the equipment—the whole room—to shifter specifications, it probably would have fallen.

The bag swung back and Graham met it with all of his frustration and a fist; not as hard as the first time, because that kind of hit was sloppy. No opponent would wait around for a fighter to regain their balance after committing all their energy into a punch that way.

He lay into the bag with all of his focus he could muster, dancing on the balls of his feet, feinting, hitting. But he couldn't shake his awareness of Alice behind him.

She was this tantalizing presence, like a source of heat, like magnetic north to his compass. It took all of his willpower to keep his attention on the bag before him.

Did he draw her that same way? Or did her bear have the same indifference to him that she seemed to? Graham reminded himself that her cool practicality really was the best practice. He didn't have anything to offer a mate.

A fist slipped and only shifter reflexes kept Graham from taking the heavy bag in the face. He lowered his hands, forcing his fingers to relax, and only then felt the sweat he'd worked up. The bag slowed in its pendulum motion and as the creak of the chains and the support beam stilled, he became aware that Alice was silent behind him.

"You're good," she said into the quiet, as if she felt compelled to fill it. "I teach wrestling, but it's a really different sport, of course. All about holds and takedowns and grapples, not so much on the hitting." She laughed nervously. "You don't want to teach middle school students how to hit. At that age, all they want to do is strike out already. They're swimming in a sea of puberty and haven't quite figured out how not to be self-centered jerks enslaved by their hormones."

Graham couldn't speak, too busy picturing what grappling Alice would be like. Those long limbs, that beautiful neck, strong fingers twined with his...

He grunted, unwrapping his hands.

"Graham..." The bench that Alice had been sitting on gave a creak as she stood.

He ought to turn and face her. It would be polite. He willed himself under control, and failed.

She was standing too close; he could feel her right behind him.

"Graham," she said again.

Graham gritted his teeth and turned. If she wanted to see what she was doing to him, then fine.

"No kissing," she said, and for a moment, Graham didn't understand. Then she was tugging his shirt up, and when he helped her get it over his head and throw it across the room, everything was clear and uncomplicated. He bent to her neck... not to kiss, but to bite, gently, then harder as she made a noise that was no part pain.

# Chapter 17

ALICE HAD NO DELUSIONS that she was any part Pretty Woman or Julia Roberts, but keeping kissing out of things seemed a sensible way to remind herself that this wasn't about romance or love.

So Graham did not kiss her.

He bit and nibbled and dragged his teeth along her skin, and licked and growled. His hands were gentle and strong, and his chest—that glorious chest—was even more beautiful than she remembered. He effortlessly raised her to a fever-pitch of need and hunger.

Her clothing followed his, and they were both touching and growling in desire. His cock was hard in her hand, his fingers were wet in her folds and played her clit like an instrument, until she was crying and begging for him.

They tried the workout bench—too narrow, the wrong height, too awkward for more than a few desperate strokes. They tried up against the wall, nearly knocking over the weights rack, then finally he was bending her over on the floor itself and entering her from behind, spreading her and biting at her neck until she gave a cry of release and he was joining her in the ecstasy with a roar of his own.

She shuddered through aftershocks as he slowed his thrusts and fell through the pulses of pleasure with her.

They collapsed to the floor and for a blissful moment, Graham cradled her in his strong arms, holding her close as their heartbeats returned to normal.

Finally he rolled away to lie beside her and Alice had to fight down her own instinct to snuggle back into his sweaty embrace.

"Where'd you learn to fight?" Alice asked, when she could form words again. "I didn't recognize your style." Mostly his style had been 'destroy the bag,' but the control and skill had been unmistakable.

The answer surprised her. "Prep school in England."

"Bullshit," Alice said, rolling her head to look at him. That was *always* a mistake, and he was still naked. "You did *not* go to prep school. And I thought you were *American*." She sat up, looking for her clothing instead of staring.

"Not bloody likely," Graham answered in a breath-taking accent, reaching for his own shirt. "Or at least, not always." His American accent was good, but now that Alice knew what she was listening for, she could hear the British beneath it.

"Well, that didn't look like proper British boxing," Alice said, in her own terrible 'I've watched a little BBC' accent as they dressed.

"It's not." That was a more Graham-like growl, too clipped to reveal any dialect. But to her surprise, he went on. "I... when I was eleven, my father died and it turned out he was badly in debt. I went from king of the school to charity case in a week, and there were a lot of kids—older kids—who were desperate to remind me what an ass I'd been and how far I'd fallen. I got good at hitting back."

Alice looked at him again, really looked at *him*, and when he accidentally looked up and met her gaze, he flinched but didn't look away.

It was a *confession*, hard-given. Alice blinked in surprise, guessing that Graham had probably never told anyone that.

*I love you*, he'd told her. And now, more than that, he was telling her he *trusted* her.

His blue eyes were so full of longing and regret. Alice wanted to reach out, to brush back the mane of his hair and feel his jaw in the palm of her hand.

But that was as dangerous as kissing and Alice could feel her defenses crumbling already.

"Why are you telling me this?" she asked quietly.

"I want..." he paused, and Alice could see him wrestling with the words. He wanted *her*, she knew with bone-deep certainty. He wanted more than he could ask. "I want to be *honest*."

*We should be honest*, she'd told him. Her own words, thrust back at her.

But she was afraid of honest. Honest terrified her.

Honest meant admitting she was falling in love with him.

# Chapter 18

GRAHAM WASN'T SURE what made him tell Alice about school, about losing his father. He hadn't intended to, not really.

He was just... so tired of trying to hide it all.

Her hazel eyes were a safe place, a haven forever.

Even if she said she didn't want *forever*.

They gazed at each other a long moment and Alice looked down first. Graham waited for her to make an excuse and flee, and was surprised when she didn't. She sat backwards on a beat-up chair and Graham settled opposite from her on a workout bench.

"My brother and I went to public school," Alice said quietly. "But kids are kids, and they can be pretty cruel. No one messed with me, but I had to bloody a few noses for my brother. I never learned... real fighting. Just a little schoolyard scrapping. But I was bigger and stronger than other kids, even before I could shift, and I didn't have to do it much."

Graham wondered if this was the place normal people made conversational noises and was glad when Alice went on without prompting.

"My brother, Andy... he's not a shifter. If he had been..." Alice's face was complicated.

Everything about Alice was complicated, however hard she tried to deny it.

After a moment, she lifted her chin. "We're being honest. My brother is sick. Really sick. He hasn't been able to work, doesn't have insurance to cover treatment, doesn't want my parents to know, even if they had any money. My parents are about to lose their house. And they don't want Andy to know. So... I'm stuck in the middle and a teacher's salary barely covers my food and the rent for my crappy apartment, so there's nothing I can do to help either of them."

Graham wasn't sure what the right response was, but "Shit," seemed as appropriate as anything.

"Sorry," she said, blinking hard to pretend she wasn't crying. "That's probably a little too much honesty for what we have. I just... haven't had anyone I could tell."

"Can I... help?" Graham had to ask, resisting the desire to pull her into his arms without asking.

Alice's mouth quirked into a wry smile; even crying, she was impossibly good looking, her face all proud planes and sun-kissed skin.

"I don't suppose you know what Scarlet's shift is?" she said, clearly expecting him to take it as a joke.

It *wasn't* a joke. Graham knew he was scowling, and hoped he had gotten the expression in place before Alice saw the underlying surprise and fear.

"How would that help?" he asked curtly, forcing his body to stay relaxed.

Alice didn't seem to notice the effect of her unexpected words, busy wiping her face and pulling herself back together. "It's crazy. Right before I left to come here, this... guy came to see me. Some big shot in an amazing suit. Mob, maybe? I don't know. No Godfather accent or anything. He gave me a business card with a number and a name, nothing else. He knew every tiny detail of my life and he offered to pay me fifty million to find out what Scarlet was. And craziest of all, I actually believe he would." She gave a wry chuckle. "Not that I have a chance in hell of cracking that egg. It's been dead-end after dead-end, and Scarlet probably thinks I'm stalking her. Or maybe flirting with her. It's been awkward."

Graham gave a gruff laugh a little too late to sound completely natural.

He was alarmed.

Deeply alarmed.

He needed to warn Scarlet...

"Don't tell anyone, okay? It's not the kind of thing I really want to explain."

Graham felt his stomach churn as his loyalties clashed. He couldn't refuse his mate's request; the weight of his lion's insistence that they honor her trust was like having the heavy bag on his shoulders, but with claws. But Scarlet should know... he *owed* her, and that weight felt equal, but with claws of guilt.

Alice was looking at him again, that way that she got, that Graham sometimes felt in his own face, like she couldn't help looking at him, like she wanted to look away but couldn't.

He couldn't deny his mate.

"Yeah," he said shortly, sealing his fate.

The relief on her face was the barest salve to the fire of his guilt.

He stood up abruptly and wasn't sure what to say. To his gratitude, Alice stood too. "Thanks," she said shyly. "I mean...

for that, and... I'm glad we're being honest, you know. It's nice to have someone... I trust."

Shy gave Alice a whole level of appeal. She usually blustered through things with a cow-catcher of confidence that Graham was beginning to understand was just a facade.

And while her strength and competence was incredibly sexy and hot, it was her vulnerability, her weakness, that did something unexpected to Graham's insides.

"I... want to be," Graham said, then got himself tangled around the grammar. "Be someone you trust, I mean...."

*But don't*, he wanted to add. *Don't trust me. Don't have faith in me. Don't believe the best of me, because it's all a lie. You were right to run...*

He should tell her the rest of *his* story, he thought, but he couldn't get the words from his mouth. He knew what she would do, and he wouldn't be able to bear her reaction. She'd be horrified. She'd be disgusted.

She'd be *afraid*.

Right now, she wasn't afraid, she was looking at him with unexpected softness and thoughtfulness.

Before Graham could figure out how to tell her the rest of what he wanted to, Alice cleared her throat uncomfortably, balled up a fist and punched him in the arm. "Anyway, thanks," she said cheerfully, not quite looking at him. "Good workout."

And just like that, she was gone.

Graham rubbed his face and threaded his fingers through his unruly hair.

For someone who wanted to keep things uncomplicated, she certainly set him on a roller coaster of emotions.

He wasn't sure how long he sat there before the phone in his pocket buzzed. Scarlet had given it to him so that she had a legitimate way to contact him, and he took it out expecting a text from her.

The number was unknown, but Graham knew who it was immediately by the content of the text:

PEOPLE ARE SNIFFING. $1000 TO KEEP QUIET.

# Chapter 19

ALICE HATED HOW SOCIALLY inept she could be, hanging behind Mary and Neal, Amber and Tony.

When they had invited her to join them on a trip across the island, she had been so eager to get out of the sleepy resort and *do* something other than think about all the things she couldn't control that she undoubtedly missed all the cues that they wouldn't really want her along. It didn't even occur to her to put together all the pieces and realize what a personal journey this was going to be.

The ride itself had started well; Neal drove the resort Jeep down the ridiculously winding, bumpy road to the airstrip they'd flow into, and they all laughed and talked about the state of the track and the incredible heat, and the island, and the wedding, and their plans to go snorkeling. From the airstrip, it was still a merry trip, over a road that was nearly but not quite as bad as the resort road, to the compound on the other side of the island.

But as they drew closer, the mood dampened, even if the sunny day did not.

When they pulled into the overgrown drive, the party was sober and quiet.

And now she was the most awkward fifth wheel since the wheel itself was invented, watching the two couples wander hand-in-hand through the abandoned compound and the charred remains of the zoo where Neal and Tony had been tortured.

The jungle was starting to spill in over the lawn around the compound. Alice could tell that it had once been neatly groomed and sharp-edged, but now it was almost blurry as brush crept in from the forest, sending tendrils of vines and shoots of roots across the unkempt grass.

The arboretum they walked solemnly through was still mostly standing, but Amber exclaimed over how damaged it was and even Alice could see that neglect had not been kind to the more delicate plants within.

"There were so many birds when I was here," Amber said thoughtfully. "Hummingbirds, and orioles, I remember."

They all stopped and listened.

"I don't hear any birds at all," Alice observed. There were insects, and frogs, but no birdsong.

The compound was even more eerie after that realization.

The house itself was largely undamaged, but had clearly been stripped and stood empty, with gaping dark windows. Here, too, jungle had started to take over. Green vines trailed up over the walls, and skinny saplings spotted the lawns and choked the gardens.

Rain had washed the worst of the soot and ash away, but the bones of the zoo behind the house were still black, twisted and warped. The wall around it looked like it had been burned to the foundations by impossible heat. No cage was whole, but some were half-standing, at least one wall ripped open and burned down on each of them.

It was a stunning display of power and Alice was awed by the sheer scope of the damage.

This was the act of someone who clearly had no intention of being caged again.

She wished she had a hand of her own to hold, watching the others cling to each other. Even though she hadn't been imprisoned or abused in this place, she could imagine what it had been like, how horrifying it would be to be caged and forced to stay in her animal form.

*No offense*, she told her bear.

Her bear was as bothered as she was. *No one is meant to be in a cage*, she said gruffly.

They found, picking through the rubble, the cell where Tony had been held.

"It wasn't that long for me," he said, with a sympathetic sidelong look at Neal, who had spent ten years in his own enclosure.

Amber clung to his arm. "I remember how it hurt you," she said fiercely. "I *remember*."

Mary said nothing, her fingers twined tight with her mate's.

They found Neal's cage next; it was little more than a few black bars striking up through concrete, and some crumbling steps.

"I tore the lock off the door when I was finally free," Neal said thoughtfully, crouching at what must have been a doorway once. "I gave it to Gizelle. I wonder if she still has it."

He spoke mechanically, like it was something distant and half-forgotten, but when Mary knelt and put her arms around him, he hunched over as if he still felt pain.

Alice retreated swiftly, knowing she was unwelcome in the moment of comfort. Amber and Tony had already returned to the arboretum and Amber was sitting on an unbroken portion of bench while Tony made her drink water and fussed about her health.

Alice wandered to the back of the zoo, over the scar of the wall, to the shaggy lawn that overlooked the sea. They were so high here that the waves were barely wrinkles below them, and the noise of surf was a distant hum. A road, half-washed out, led steeply down to a long dock and a half-moon of beach.

There were burned bars and chunks of rubble even here, as if they had been thrown from the zoo in a fiery explosion. Alice tested one of the dark concrete slabs with her hand, expecting the black to rub off on her like fresh soot, and was surprised when it came away clean. She sat on it, pulled her knees up against her chest, and wished she weren't thinking of Graham.

He might not say much, she thought, but his solid presence beside her would have been comforting.

She glanced back at the zoo, where Mary and Neal were sitting together in the bones of his cage. He had his arms wrapped around her and she was murmuring in his ear as she held him.

She could have that, it suddenly occurred to Alice.

She could have that unwavering support, that true bond, that unflinching comfort.

Graham loved her.

It was more than his blurted first words, it was more than the way he had rushed to protect her from Gizelle's mate. It was the way he gazed at her when he couldn't help it. It was the trust he cautiously extended her, like he was afraid of being pushed away... with good reason considering her insistence that there was nothing between them but animal need.

She could have the same security and partnership that Mary and Amber had found, that same happiness.

All she had to do was accept that she loved him in return.

# Chapter 20

"WE'VE GOT HIM," JENNY said triumphantly, pulling her phone from her ear. "We've got Grant Lyons!"

Graham, who had been planning to sneak straight past the kitchen and go to bed hungry rather than face the smirks and pity and questions that the rest of the staff would have, froze in the doorway.

He wished, not for the first time, that he'd fought harder to get the servants quarters that Breck had claimed when they first moved into The Den. At the time, Breck had needed the private entrance much more than Graham did.

Now, every eye from the living room and kitchen was on Jenny—and because Graham was right behind her, his entrance was at the edge of the spotlight.

"I've got a contact who has Lyons' current name and location, and he's agreed to sell it to us. I'm wiring him the money right now." Jenny had her phone in her hands and was clearly starting the transaction.

The rest of the staff murmured in excitement and interest.

"I wonder if this is what Tony feels like doing spy work," Jenny said gleefully. "I can hear the James Bond theme in my head."

"Stop."

Graham's voice surprised even him and if he had been at the edge of a metaphorical spotlight before, he was now in the blinding center of it. Breck and Darla were standing at the sink still holding the dishes they had been washing and drying together. Saina and Bastian were sitting at the kitchen bar, Travis leaning at the end of it. Wrench and Lydia were in the living room sitting together on the couch near Laura, and Tex had been closing the windows. Someone had muted the television at Jenny's exclamation.

"He's not, you know, a shining example of morality," Jenny said apologetically, looking at Graham. "But I understand he's good for his word. I got his information from a guy Tony knows, so it should be pretty safe."

Graham laughed humorlessly. "Johnny Ace *is* good for his word... unless someone else is willing to pay more."

Jenny blinked at him. "How did you know his name?" she asked slowly. "I only got this information this afternoon."

Graham looked around the room.

These were his friends.

These were *Graham's* friends.

They trusted *Graham*. They thought he was a good guy.

If he was honest with them, if he told them the truth, they'd know better. He'd destroy every fragile thing he'd found here, salting the earth of their friendship.

Secrets rose up in his throat, threatening to suffocate him, and he hated the taste of them.

He fingered the phone in his pocket and pulled it out. "Because the rat bastard asked me for money *not* to tell you."

They all stared at him, not daring to put the pieces together.

"I... don't understand," Jenny finally said.

She didn't *want* to understand, Graham knew.

Darla gave a little inhale of revelation, loud in the quiet room, and Graham closed his eyes.

"I'm Grant Lyons," he growled. "I'm Grant Lyons," he said louder.

It was one of the worst moments of his life.

"Why didn't you tell us?" Travis asked quietly.

"Does Scarlet know?" Bastian demanded.

"Oh, *Graham*." That was Lydia, sounding shocked and sorrowed.

Wrench gave a low growl.

"Do we have to call you m'lord?" Breck asked.

Graham opened his eyes in time to see Darla elbow the waiter in the side.

"It's a valid question," Breck protested. "Weren't the Lyons landed lords?"

"Why didn't you say something when you realized you could buy the resort?" Jenny demanded, sounding understandably put out.

"With what money?" Graham countered, angry. "I don't have a penny. And yes, Scarlet knows. She's known all along. She's in no position to come up with three hundred and fifty *million*. She's facing pretty certain bankruptcy already. Jubilee Grant's lawsuit came through, and she... didn't want to spoil Neal and Mary's wedding by letting them know."

Apparently, coming clean meant coming *completely* clean. Graham made himself snap his mouth shut before he said even more.

"Little late for that, *Grant*," Travis muttered sympathetically.

Graham turned, to find that the wedding party had come quietly through the open door behind him, and they were staring at him with the looks of shock and betrayal that he had expected.

He had eyes only for Alice, who was standing behind the others, the disillusionment in her face like a blade.

"So much for honesty," she said coldly, and she turned on her heel and stomped out.

Then it really was the worst moment of Graham's life.

# Chapter 21

ALICE TURNED BLINDLY on the path and ran, grinding her teeth and wishing herself anywhere else.

She'd told him everything, and he'd told her half-truths.

*I want to be honest,* he'd said. *It's nice to have someone to trust,* she'd told him.

And he wasn't even Graham Long.

Alice came to another fork in the path and jogged uphill, because it was harder, because she wanted the clean sweat of hard work to wash away the ugly anger and resentment and betrayal that she was feeling.

What could she trust of what he'd told her? What part of it was real and what part was the mask that he'd shown everyone?

It didn't make her feel any better that he'd been lying to everyone.

Everyone except Scarlet. *Scarlet* knew. And if Scarlet knew about Graham...

The path ended in a high wall and a closed gate marked "KEEP OUT" in red letters. Alice snarled, and turned to find somewhere else to run, then caught a whiff of Graham and knew he'd followed her.

She waited.

He wasn't running, he was walking slowly, and by the time he got to the gate, Alice had worked herself into a fury.

"You know what Scarlet is," she accused him, when he finally rounded the last corner and wearily approached.

"You knew what she was the whole time, and you knew what it would mean for me, that I could save my family. You *lied* to me. I *trusted* you."

Did he understand how rare her trust was?

Graham didn't answer, only went to the gate, opened it and went in without saying a word.

Alice hesitated a moment, then followed him.

For a moment, her anger was washed away in surprise. They walked into a garden, a beautiful, riotous, protected little area of green glory. An open greenhouse lay in one direction, uncovered beds, groaning in flowers and fruit, in the other. Jungle towered above it on the island side, open fields to the ocean side. Even in the darkness, it was gorgeous.

And it smelled... like home.

This was Graham's haven, she realized. The forbidden garden, his secret place.

But she wasn't ready to forgive him, or accept this gift as any kind of compensation for his lies and deception.

"Why didn't you tell me about Scarlet?" she demanded, only a few steps into the garden. She turned and glared at Graham, not letting herself drink in the peacefulness of the plants around them. She didn't want peacefulness, she wanted Graham to suffer some fraction of the agony she was feeling.

"Her secrets aren't mine to tell," Graham growled, in that low voice that masked accents.

"I might have accepted that," Alice snarled. "But you let me believe you didn't *know*."

Graham was silent. Insufferably silent.

"You lied about who you are," she went on, hating the silence worse than the lies. "You lied to me and talked about trust and honesty, and I don't know how I'm supposed to ever believe you about anything again."

"I'm sorry..." Graham started to say.

But Alice didn't want an apology any more than she wanted peace.

She was angry, and hurting, and she wanted to *fight* him, because she didn't know what else to do.

"You're only sorry you got *caught*," Alice hurled back at him. "You would have cheerfully continued to deceive me... for how long? Until I left after Mary and Neal's wedding? What if I'd decided to quit my job and stay here with you? Would you have let me sacrifice my whole *world* for a complete fiction?"

"I wouldn't have..."

"How can I believe anything you say!" Alice snapped, hating his gentleness, resenting his calm. "I don't know what you would have, what you might have, I only know what you *did*. What you *said*. How you *lied*. I told you everything. You let me believe you were being honest with me."

She was being impossible, she knew, and that was the very worst part. She was the one who had pushed him away, held him at arm's length. She was the one who had tried to deny that their bond was anything more than sexual need. *No kissing*, she'd told him, as if that had protected her heart in the slightest.

"I actually fell in love with you!" she railed at him, the pain in her chest like a band being tightened. "Until ten minutes ago, I thought maybe we could make something work, that there really was something here! Something *real*!"

"Don't," Graham said, sounding angry at last. "Don't love me!"

Alice was out of words, out of breath, out of the fury that had carried her this far; it was leaking out of her with the tears on her face.

Graham seemed to have absorbed all of it. "You want *my* secrets? You want to know the whole truth, who I really am?" he threatened.

Alice stared at him, not sure what to do with the emptiness in her chest or the silence in her throat.

"I'm a fighter, I'm a killer. I told you the truth about school, and I got recruited soon after to fight in an underground cage fighting ring. It was all shifters, and it was a fight in human form until one of the fighters shifted in sheer survival instinct. You know how you get shifters to take animal form? You hurt them. You hurt them so bad, they have to shift, they can't help themselves. Ask Tony, or Neal. Beehag had it down to an art."

Graham was speaking between gritted teeth, his sides heaving like he'd just run the length of the resort.

"I was *good* at hurting people. Really good at it."

Alice didn't doubt it.

Then Graham stepped forward, a sharp, aggressive move designed to frighten her.

"And I liked it," Graham hissed, close to her face. "I liked to hurt them."

## Chapter 22

IT WAS OUT THERE. IT couldn't be taken back. She knew who he really was now, and that was it.

Graham couldn't hold his angry facade for long, not in the face of Alice's foolish bravery as she gazed back at him wordlessly. She was too beautiful to bear, too courageous to endure.

"You should go," he said, stepping back and turning away. "I won't bother you again."

But she didn't go. "Why did you go to prison?" Her voice was quiet and firm.

Graham was done with lies and secrets. He would answer any question she asked.

"I killed a man."

He could have stopped there. He could have let her assume it was just an accident, could have stuck to half-truths like he always did. He could have forced her to ask the questions. Instead, he went on, continuing to stand looking away.

"He was a good fighter, strong and fast, light on his feet and well-trained. Not the best I'd ever been up against, but... good. I... thought he might have been a big cat shifter."

Had he really? Had he really had no doubts at the beginning of the fight?

"He fought hard, snapped my wrist before I got his collar bone broken and turned the tide of the fight. But he never gave up, never... never begged for mercy... never asked..."

*Grant* had begged.

*Shift*, he'd hissed, hearing the man's rib break at his hit. *Shift and concede the fight.*

*Give up,* he'd pleaded, when he dislocated his opponent's shoulder. How much abuse could he take?

*Shift*, he'd shouted, over the crowd's cheers and jeers.

*Shift*! he'd beseeched, holding the man's broken body in his arms, not sure how he hadn't surrendered to his animal instinct long before.

Then Graham finally realized why he hadn't, as the light in the man's blazing eyes slowly flickered out.

"He wasn't a shifter," Graham said. He was not sure when he had dropped to his knees, hands making fists in the gravel. "He was just a human that they'd put in a cage with me."

Behind him, Alice gave a hiss of dismay.

"I *tortured* him," Graham admitted to the strawberries before him. "I begged him to shift... but he *couldn't*. The stuff they classified in my file? It was what I did to him. How badly I hurt him. It was slaughter, it wasn't manslaughter."

"What did you do then?" Alice asked quietly. She must be horrified. It was a wonder she was still there.

"The fight coordinator was a lovely bloke by the name of Cyrus Angres. He'd been setting these fights up for a couple of years, and he was afraid that the usual show was getting... stale. I realized he'd done it knowingly, set me up to kill that man for money, and it took six guys to pull me off him. I got away, went straight to a bobby I knew in London who was a shifter and told him everything. It went to the top of International Shifter Affairs. The whole ring went under, I got a reduced sentence for manslaughter, all the details of the guy's death marked out with black pen... and afterwards I got a new identity from Johnny Ace to start over in America with."

"As Graham Long, gardener."

"Gardening ran in my family," Graham said numbly. "When Scarlet found me, she was just like Jenny, hoping I had money to restart the resort; she only had about half of what she needed raised. All she found was a broke, broken, bottom-of-the-barrel groundskeeper at a half-rate golf course in Florida. She... could have left me where she found me, it would have been a lot easier. But she made me come here, gave me purpose, showed me how to start over."

Alice's feet crunched over the gravel and she sat down on the rock edge of the strawberry bed facing Graham. "I can't picture Scarlet in Florida," she said thoughtfully, as if *that* was the surprising part of the whole sordid story.

"She wasn't," Graham said quietly. "She can't leave the island. She got my phone number, wired me a plane ticket, convinced me to use it."

"Graham..."

"Grant," he corrected. "Grant Lyons. Murderer."

"*Graham*," Alice insisted. "You are Graham Long now, and it was Graham Long that I fell in love with."

He put his forehead down on the rock edge of the strawberry bed next to her. "Grant is still who I am," he said plaintively. "And you don't understand. I liked to hurt people. I *liked* it."

"Bullshit," Alice said flatly, to his surprise.

She didn't get it, Graham thought in despair. "You don't know..."

# Chapter 23

ALICE HAD NOT BELIEVED that there could be anything more devastating and distracting than Graham's—Grant's—bare chest.

She was wrong.

When Graham spoke—really spoke, in a confessional rush of words—he had the sexiest British accent that Alice had ever heard. The extra 'r's, the clear 't's, the drawn out 'oo's... move over Tom Hiddleston.

She had to force herself to listen to his words, and not just drown in his voice.

He believed he was a monster, she realized as he spoke. A terrible person who did terrible things and liked them.

But Alice knew better. She knew Graham from the bottom of his soul to each gentle fingertip. She knew his heart.

"You don't know..." he said softly.

"I *do*. I watch this happen to kids in sports all the time. They don't love the sport, they only love being good at it," Alice said firmly. "They get so wrapped up in what people expect them to do with a talent that they start thinking of themselves only in terms of that skill. They define themselves by what they're good at, and they think that they enjoy it because it's the only time they feel worth anything. That's not enjoyment, that's *entrapment*."

She knelt beside him, putting a hand hesitantly on his shoulder. "Enjoying a fight where you get to be good at something, and there are people cheering you on, and you know that all your injuries and theirs will heal up in a couple of days... that's not the same as liking to *hurt* people. You *knew* the difference, and you went out there and flipped tables because you were tricked into an unfair fight that only had one ending."

Her arm slid around him and Graham turned in her embrace to lay his head on her shoulder. She tangled her fingers in his hair and rested her head on his.

It was so comfortable, so natural, to hold him like that; Alice didn't even mind the sharp gravel pressing into her knees.

"Graham," she started.

"Grant," he corrected firmly into her collarbone. His arms had crept around her, and he was pressed up close against her for comfort.

"I'll call you what you want," Alice said just as firmly. "But you are not the Grant you've convinced yourself you are."

"Who am I, then?" he asked, drawing back to look her in the eyes.

*Mine*, Alice wanted to say.

*Ours*, her bear was growling.

Alice couldn't say either of those things out loud, so she simply leaned forward and kissed him.

After a split second of surprise, Graham opened his mouth and kissed her back desperately, taking her face in his hands.

She'd been right not to kiss him before, Alice decided. It was like baring her soul to him; it undid her. She was helpless in his hands, utterly lost to his taste and his tongue and his hungry mouth.

Every inch of him was irresistible. Both of them rose to their feet, still kissing, as Graham lifted her shirt from her. She tried to get his shirt off while he was trying to unclip her bra, and they quickly realized they were working to cross-purposes and stripped off their own clothing.

For a moment, they simply stood close, not touching, just gazing at each other. But not for long; Alice couldn't keep her eyes, or her fingers, from his beautiful shoulders, or his broad chest, or his amazing jaw, and she gave a little gasp as Graham stepped forward, his cock pressing just where it should as he kissed her again.

Alice didn't think that he could unravel her more, but the second kiss was deeper, and there was no clothing to keep his intoxicating skin from her starving fingers.

She gave a gasp of surprise as he suddenly wrapped his arms around her and lifted her to lay her back, directly into one of the beds of strawberries.

Then his weight was over her like a shield and he was pressing into her as Alice spread her legs in invitation. She was impossibly wet, he was impossibly hard, and when he slid into her there was a moment of pleasure so intense and intimate that Alice had to cry out in surrender.

For a heartbeat, he held there, buried inside her, then he bent to kiss her, and began to thrust, slowly, gently, deeper every stroke, and Alice felt like he was drawing her up on an unbreakable thread.

She kissed him back, arching up, wrapping her legs around him because there was no such thing as close enough, no place inside of her that didn't want him.

When she found shuddering release, crying out in pleasure she didn't want to deny, she opened her eyes and found him gazing at her in wonder and need.

Impulsively, she wrapped one leg around his and turned him onto his back, barely staying coupled as they rolled. She lifted his arms above his head and leaned on his forearms, pinning him, riding him, taking him deeper than she'd ever thought was possible. He let her hold him down, hips rising to meet her strokes, until she was falling into a second whirlpool of pleasure.

He broke free of her hands then and wrapped his arms tight around her, holding her closer and closer, until he was spilling his ecstasy into her, groaning and growling near her ear.

Neither one of them let go this time, continuing to embrace as their heartbeats finally slowed and they could catch their breath again.

She was never going to be able to eat the berries again without evoking the memories of Graham. The scent of bruised leaves and squashed berries and disturbed earth was heady and strong; Alice felt like she'd just made love in a dessert.

"Poor, crushed strawberries," Alice finally said.

She giggled. "The gardener is going to be so pissed..."

Below her, Graham made a rumbling noise. For a moment, Alice wondered if she was too heavy to keep lying on him, then realized he was laughing. It was the most beautiful sound she'd ever heard, vibrating through her entire body and she chortled with him helplessly.

"Alice," he said, sitting up with his arms still around her. His laughter stilled. "Alice..."

If his voice in confession was disturbing, his voice saying her name struck some raw nerve inside of her and Alice suddenly felt like her world was dropping away. "I don't know," she said to the question he wasn't asking. "I don't know what this means. I don't know what it changes." She plucked a flattened strawberry from her shoulder blade and shook it off her fingers.

"Scarlet..." he started to say.

"Don't tell me what she is," Alice stopped him. "I can't ask you to do that. You were right that it's not your secret to give, and I shouldn't have asked you."

Graham gave a little shudder. "*You* were right that I know what she is, though. She's been a friend of my family for decades. She was my grandfather's... partner."

"Don't tell me what she is," Alice repeated. "Not like this." Then, as if she was compelled to ask, "Partner, like... lovers?"

"No, though I think that she may have loved him. She was technically his secretary, but she was much more to our family than that. The resort was supposed to be hers, when he built it."

"Where did she get the rest of the money?" Alice asked, when he was quiet for a moment.

"She didn't," Graham explained. "This *is* only half of what the resort was meant to be. She scrapped the plans for a little community that was meant to be located over on this corner of the island, hoping that if the resort took off, she'd be able to add it on later."

"And now?"

Graham sighed. "Now she's going to lose it all."

Alice shivered in the cooling evening breeze and stood up to find her clothes. She tossed Graham's pants at him. "She doesn't have to..." she said thoughtfully, pulling her shirt on without a bra.

Graham, as appealing shimmying into his pants as he'd been getting out of them, scowled at her. "What do you mean?"

"You've got some flush clients who love this place," Alice suggested. "Isn't Gizelle's mate a billionaire? Hasn't royalty stayed here? What if Scarlet ran a crowdfunding thing? Like, a timeshare program, but without the vulture salespeople, to raise enough money to buy it outright. They'd *have* to sell it to you if you came up with the cash, right?"

Graham stared at her. "They'd have to sell it to me, but they're listing the island as a whole; we'd have to buy the entire thing. They want three hundred and fifty *million* dollars."

Alice tried not to choke on the very idea of that kind of money.

"That would be... a lot of crowdfunding," Alice conceded. "And I think I have a squashed strawberry in my underwear."

# Chapter 24

WHEN GRAHAM AND ALICE returned to The Den, there was no real way to get back in to his room privately, or sneak to the shower, or pretend that nothing had happened, so they didn't try. The rest of the staff was already gathered in the living area, and the hum of conversation that they'd heard through the open windows came to a stop when Graham cracked the door.

Everyone politely pretended they weren't craning to see if it was Graham alone, or if Alice with him, except Breck, who turned completely around on the couch, propped his chin on both hands, and greeted them cheerfully.

"Welcome back, your lordship!"

Darla gave a chiding murmur that couldn't hide her amusement and Laura threw a pillow at him.

"There's a bottle of wine on the counter," Mary pointed out.

"Oh, good," Alice said, opening cabinets at random until she found the glasses. "You want one?"

Graham shook his head.

While Alice filled her tumbler, the others discretely rearranged themselves on the chairs and couches so that the only free spots were together.

Graham stalked to take one of them, Alice following. He settled gingerly into place, wishing he had taken a glass of wine simply to have something to do with his hands. Alice flopped down beside him, pushing her sandals off with each opposite foot and tucking her legs up under her. They weren't quite touching.

Everyone *grinned*.

"We've been talking about how we might save the resort," Jenny said quickly. "We're thinking about trying to raise the money ourselves. If we can, they have to sell it to you."

"If you're in," Laura added.

Graham grunted.

"Great minds think alike," Alice said. "We were just talking about that."

Jenny had her computer in her lap. "We're definitely going to ask Conall, and Magnolia. Laura and I are still fighting legal battles over the life insurance policy that Fred stole when our parents died, but Fred's estate is running out of appeals to make, so we should get it soon. It will be a pretty good drop in the bucket."

"I... have a few things of value," Bastian said uncomfortably.

"You can't sell your hoard," Saina said to him, dismayed.

Bastian took her hands in his. "It's not worth a lot," he said, looking embarrassed. "But this is greater treasure." He looked around at the others in The Den. "If the resort isn't here, I don't have a hoard worth having."

Saina kissed him. "I know people who can fence anything we need."

"I have some jewelry," Lydia said thoughtfully. "Nothing spectacular, but some of it is gold."

"I've got a watch," Tex said. "It might have some value as an antique."

Jenny was busily tapping onto her keyboard as everyone volunteered what they could and guessed prices that seemed pathetic compared to the monstrous number they were aiming for.

"What about Scarlet?" Alice asked. "She must know some well-to-do people to ask." Graham wondered if she was thinking about the mysterious offer for the information on Scarlet, and her own dire straits. Fifty million would go a long ways.

Lydia, sitting nearly in Wrench's lap on the crowded couch, shook her head. "Scarlet told us not to look for Grant Lyons."

"To protect Graham," Alice reminded them. "But you all know now."

"Your…" Darla smothered Breck with the throw pillow before he could finish the *lordship* part.

"We were thinking we would try to do it quietly and surprise her," Laura said. "She's so private and proud, I think she might try to stop us."

Graham knew she would, and his nod caught Laura's attention.

"Are you in?" Laura asked him.

"I've got nothing of value," Graham apologized.

"The sale has to be in your name," Laura pointed out. "You'd be the owner."

"Do I have to be?" Graham asked with a scowl. "Can't I sign it away to Scarlet?"

"Yeah, you can do that," Jenny said confidently, to his relief. "That's quite straight-forward."

"Good," Travis said with a grin. "I don't want Graham the Grouch calculating my bonuses."

"Are you bleeding?" Lydia asked suddenly, leaning over to Alice.

Alice looked down at her leg. "Nope," she said, peeling the red spot off. "Strawberry."

"I thought I smelled strawberries!" Amber laughed. "I couldn't figure out why."

"I think there's one in your hair, Graham," Mary observed shyly.

"Hypocrite!" Breck exclaimed in outrage. "All the grief you give us for damaging your precious flower gardens and you're off rolling in the strawberry beds! Flowers are one thing, but we *eat* those."

Everyone stared in wonder at Graham and it took him a long moment to realize that it was because he was laughing.

# Chapter 25

ALICE SPENT A LONG moment after she woke with her eyes closed, too comfortable to move, clinging to sweet, peaceful sleep.

Graham had an arm draped over her and one foot hooked around her ankle. A single sheet was more than enough warmth for the morning; already the temperature was rising as the sun came up over the island.

Despite a shower, Alice could still smell strawberries, and it filled her with unexpected contentment.

This was where she belonged, she thought, and the idea was so unexpected that her eyes flew open in alarm and her peace shattered.

Graham stirred as she sat up and, in a smooth, practiced way, rolled out of bed and began getting dressed as if on autopilot. Alice was watching him as he woke up enough to realize what was different, turning back to look at her in amazement and confusion.

She gave him a crooked smile as he stood there, frozen with one leg in his pants.

"Morning," she said wryly.

He scowled at her; clearly this was his reaction to any surprise. "Good morning," he growled, stuffing the other leg into his khakis.

Alice pushed off the sheet and was delighted to watch Graham nearly fall over staring at her. "So... ah... I told the girls I'd work on the bachelorette party with them today."

Graham managed to save his balance and, still shirtless, he walked around the bed as she stood up. "Alice..." he started.

Guessing his train of thought, Alice was swift to say, "I don't know what this all means long term, okay? I have a job I love, and problems I can't solve living here at Shifting Sands." Damn his chest... even with her body humming and satiated, Alice wanted nothing more than to lay her hands over those gorgeous muscles and push him back down on the bed. Instead, she reached for her clothing and began to get dressed.

Did he look hurt? Alice couldn't guess behind the frown on his face or his stony silence, but just the idea of it made her stomach clench. "It's not that I don't..." she wasn't going to say that she loved him again. That would only make it harder to leave. "I'm really... I don't want you to think..."

*She didn't want to leave.*

Graham and his naked chest closed the distance between them and he put his hand gently on either side of her face. This made it very challenging to continue getting dressed and Alice stopped trying.

"You don't have to know," Graham said softly. "We can take it a day at a time."

Alice surprised herself with a rush of warmth and desire. "Yeah," she agreed breathlessly. And that was as long as she could resist his shirtless self, slipping her arms up around his broad shoulders to kiss him. In short order, they had peeled each other out of the clothing they'd just put on and he was showing her how to make the most of those days that they were taking one at a time.

Hours later, freshly showered and *still* somehow smelling of strawberries, Alice found herself at the buffet.

She took a second baked chicken leg from the buffet, considered putting it back, and then took a third one out of spite.

Spite, or appetite, she thought; she'd skipped breakfast to shamelessly make Graham late for work.

She considered a fourth chicken leg and decided that she should save room for dessert instead. Graham had mentioned a fresh crop of strawberries...

Mary and Amber had their heads together with Laura and Jenny at one of the larger tables and Alice thought they were waving her over until she realized they were trying to catch the attention of the woman behind her.

"Magnolia," Laura called. "Could we talk to you a moment?"

Magnolia looked like she had never turned down a fourth chicken leg in her life. Or possibly a tenth.

They sat down opposite from each other at the table, Magnolia with a tray heaping with fine cheeses and fruit and fluffy sweetbread, Alice with her pile of chicken legs and a four-inch-high sandwich. Jenny had her laptop open in front of her and was busily typing.

"I'm Alice." Alice was never sure how long to wait for someone else to introduce her, and generally did so herself.

"Magnolia," the other woman greeted with a gracious smile and an elegant fingershake. "You're Graham's mate."

Alice blinked at her, momentarily speechless. No one else had said as much aloud after the first terrible day, and it felt weird to hear it. "Yeah," she agreed. *Mate* was as good a classification as anything, she decided. She didn't feel like a *girlfriend*.

Magnolia smiled at her and Alice thought dazedly that she'd never been at the receiving end of a smile that lovely and sincere before. "I'm delighted to meet you," the woman said. "Graham needs a little goodness in his life like you."

No one had ever called Alice 'a little goodness' before, but she supposed that if anyone could, it was Magnolia, who probably outweighed her by two hundred pounds.

"What did you need, darling?" Magnolia asked Jenny.

Jenny lowered her voice and they all leaned into the table when she did. "It's a bit of a delicate question," she confessed. "But we're trying to raise money to buy the island. We've recently found out that Graham is Grant Lyons, and he gets first refusal of a sale by contract. If we can get enough people together, we'd be able to buy it outright and we'd never have to worry about Beehag breaking the lease or selling it out from under us."

She went on hastily. "I'm drawing up contracts that would give investors a stake in the resort, and we can talk about terms and such, but... is that something you'd be interested in? Something you could help with?"

Magnolia looked thoughtful, but not entirely happy.

"Is there a reason that it isn't Scarlet herself telling me this?" she asked suspiciously.

"She doesn't know," Laura admitted. "It's a long shot, but we're trying to surprise her."

Magnolia laughed in delight. "I love a good surprise," she said eagerly. Then she sobered. "But I'm afraid there's very little I can pledge. My money comes from a trust that I have limited access to. I don't have any savings I can reach, and my lease payment here is almost my entire monthly payout."

Everyone at the table gave a sigh of regret. "I understand," Jenny said. "We'll keep looking."

Magnolia inspected a be-ringed hand thoughtfully. "I have some jewelry. It won't be much compared to the asking price of the island, but it's yours, no contract needed. Scarlet *should* own the island."

"Saina's offered to fence anything we can get together," Laura said gratefully. "Bastian's got her looking for buyers for part of his hoard. We'll put our insurance settlement in, if we can ever get it litigated. Fred managed to get a fancy law firm in New York to defend his estate, so there have been problems."

"We're also writing to all the survivors of Beehag's zoo," Mary explained. "They all owe Scarlet for her hospitality, and this would be a great way to repay it."

"Tony is taking a bit of a risk giving us their contact information, but I don't think any of them will mind. It's not likely that any of them are sitting on millions of dollars," Amber said wryly, "but there's always some hope."

"And little pledges *will* add up," Jenny added optimistically.

*Fifty million would add a lot, too*, Alice thought wryly. But she didn't like to think about that, or the fact that Graham had the key to that payout... or the fact that even if she knew it, she wasn't sure she could betray Scarlet's secret.

Even for fifty million dollars.

Even to save her brother and her parents.

Her chicken legs were suddenly looking a lot less appealing.

Alice thought about the pathetic scrap book she'd tried to use as a cover for asking Scarlet questions. "Scarlet's pretty private and proud. She's probably not going to be really happy that you're sending her business failures to everyone she's ever helped."

The others looked at her with expressions of mixed guilt, skepticism, and curiosity and Alice wished she hadn't said anything at all. She took a fierce bite of chicken leg.

"I mean... not that I know her well," she said uncomfortably around her food. "But I guess *I'd* be pretty embarrassed."

"That's why she wouldn't do it herself," Jenny said thoughtfully. "But if we can buy the island, it would be worth it. I think she'd understand."

Alice nodded. "Yeah, you're probably right."

"Besides," Laura added, "it's not like this is actually a failure of *Scarlet's*. She was kind enough to take all those shifters in, knowing that it was her bottom line that would pay for it. It was... a failure of kindness, not business."

"Oo," Jenny said. "Failure of kindness. I like that. I'm stealing it." She typed feverishly into her laptop.

"This is a lovely thing you're doing," Magnolia said, eating gracefully. "I'll help out any way I can."

Alice finished her meal as quickly as she could, wishing she had an ounce of the other woman's grace.

## Chapter 26

GRAHAM POLITELY AVERTED his eyes when Gizelle opened her door naked.

"Is Conall here?" he asked gruffly.

Gizelle cocked her head at him. "He's always somewhere," she said, not offering to get her mate or put on clothing.

"Can I talk to him? I might need your help."

A smile bloomed over Gizelle's face. "I like to help."

She scampered away into the bedroom, leaving the cottage door open behind her.

Graham hung at the doorway for a moment, not sure if it was an invitation to enter or not, and finally went in and gingerly took a seat in one of the plush chairs.

When Gizelle reappeared, Graham was relieved to see that she was dressed. He stood as Conall came into the little living room and they briefly shook hands before sitting opposite each other. Gizelle curled up beside the Irish elk shifter, a hand casually resting on his bare arm so that he could hear and didn't have to rely on lip reading.

"Is there a problem?" Conall asked, eyeing the folder that Graham was holding.

"I hope this is actually a solution," Graham said. He leaned forward to hand Conall the folder over the sturdy wooden coffee table. "Jenny is working out the finer details, but we're hoping you're interested in buying an interest in the island and saving Shifting Sands Resort."

Conall took the folder and opened it with a frown. "I'm surprised that Scarlet isn't approaching me with this herself."

Graham grimaced. "Scarlet doesn't know. We're only in the early stages of trying to figure out if this is even feasible."

"You look like you drew the short straw," Conall observed, glancing up from the paperwork in the folder with a hint of a smile.

Graham chuckled. He and Conall had quietly become good friends. Others joked that it was because Conall, deaf, didn't have to worry about lip reading Graham because he never said anything.

Graham had volunteered to come talk to the Irish elk shifter, mostly because he wanted to confess who he was personally, rather than letting the information get to Conall by the grapevine.

"My real name is Grant Lyons," he admitted. "I am the blood heir of Aaric Lyons, the man who started the resort forty years ago. It's in the lease contract that I get first right of refusal on a purchase of the island. If we can raise the funds, we can buy the island at their public asking price, even if there are other buyers."

Conall looked at him quizzically, but didn't question the revelation of Graham's true identity.

Gizelle, on the other hand, was nodding sagely. "You're from the lion who came before," she said, as if it made perfect sense. Then she added, "I will still call you Graham."

"I would like that," Graham told her gravely.

Conall nodded thoughtfully as he flipped through the paperwork that Jenny had sent with Graham. "I'll have to consult with my financial advisor, of course. I'm quite interested, but... this is the asking price? Three hundred and fifty million?"

Graham nodded. It was a stunning amount of money. "The sale is for the entire island as a package, almost twenty thousand acres, including Beehag's compound, the dock, the airstrip, and the resort. That's the price set by an independent auditor. On top of that, Darla's mother has filed the lawsuit we were expecting. More than a million."

Conall closed the folder. "I am only a paper billionaire," he said frankly. "I have some assets I could liquidate, but most of my wealth is tied up in my business, which is still on the market. We've had two buyers now who seemed interested, got as far as earnest money, and then bailed out under mysterious circumstances. If I were a superstitious man, I might suspect a conspiracy."

"But you're interested," Graham said in relief.

Conall looked at Gizelle, who had her legs up the back of the couch, leaning her head backwards off the seat staring upside down at Graham, hand still carefully on Conall so that he could hear.

"We belong here," he said soberly. "I don't relish the idea of anyone else getting their hands on the resort with the ability to throw us out or disrupt our peace. I've seen some of the prospective buyers that Beehag has brought through, and it's clear that he's working to uproot Scarlet from the island. He's involved with someone subtle and clever, who is willing to use unorthodox methods. My interest in the resort is selfish and personal, but no less sincere. I'll make some phone calls and get you a concrete pledge. If I could do the full amount, I would, and I genuinely hope you are able to raise the rest."

Graham bowed his head. "Thank you," he said, rising and shaking Conall's hand. "I appreciate it."

Gizelle let go of Conall as he stood to shake Graham's hand and Graham caught the brief flinch when she did. "Wait!" she said suddenly, and she vaulted over the couch and disappeared into the bedroom.

"Has she seen Neal yet?" Graham thought to ask, making sure Conall was watching him.

Conall shook his head. "She does things in her own time," he said patiently. "I've had a chance to talk with him a little, though. Good man."

Gizelle came back out of the bedroom. She was holding a tablet and a pair of earphones. "Can these save Scarlet?" she asked shyly.

Graham exchanged a look with Conall, not sure how to answer. She hadn't been touching him, and had been facing Graham, so she had to turn and repeat herself to her mate, adding, "It's my fault."

"What's your fault, sweetheart?" Conall asked, concerned.

"When it rains," Gizelle answered calmly. "And the cage breaks."

Conall frowned and shook his head. "You don't need to give up your tablet," he assured her, ignoring the rest of her nonsense. "It is kind of you to offer, but you can help me talk with my accountant—that will be a big help."

"You could help us distract Scarlet," Graham suggested, inspiration striking. "It's a secret, that we're trying to raise the money. Could you help keep her from finding out?"

Gizelle smiled like the moon. "I'm good at keeping secrets!" she said enthusiastically. "Oh! Secrets! We haven't finished reading *The Secret Garden*! I will ask her to!"

"She'd like that," Graham said sincerely to her back as she fled from the house, still clutching her tablet.

Conall smiled fondly after her, then scowled self-consciously when he caught Graham watching him.

"I didn't mean this exact moment," Graham said, with an apologetic shrug.

"Like I said, she does things in her own time," Conall said briefly.

They shook hands again and Graham went to take the news to the rest of the staff.

# Chapter 27

"HEY, HANDSOME!" ALICE called as she approached.

Graham stopped raking and leaned on the handle like a Greek statue, his mane of hair golden in the sunlight.

"I keep making you late for work, so I brought you lunch from the buffet," she said cheerfully.

Graham smiled slowly. "Thanks," he said gratefully. "Scarlet read us the riot act at the staff meeting today. She had a lot to say about how romance and weddings shouldn't be keeping us from doing our jobs, and how she can't run a business if we insist on treating it like a summer camp."

Alice gave a laughing groan as she handed Graham the plates with the sandwich she'd put together. "She's probably in a terrible mood."

"Everyone who can is avoiding her," Graham agreed.

It wasn't only the upcoming wedding that was distracting everyone, of course... everyone was doing what they could to get money towards the purchase of the resort, and if the outstanding balance was still intimidating, it was encouraging to watch the total slowly rising as they got in touch with more of Scarlet's previous guests. Alice had been flabbergasted when Jenny gleefully announced that the Empress of Atlantis had dropped a cool five million into the pot. She wasn't sure which part of the statement astonished her the most: Empress, Atlantis, or *five million*.

"Next you're going to tell me a royal *unicorn* family is making a donation," Alice had scoffed in disbelief, trying to think of anything more unbelievable.

"Already did," Jenny had laughed, pointing to a respectable pledge in the ledger. "Not royalty, quite, but English nobility."

In ten days, they had raised more than half of the impossible goal.

She and Graham sat together on the bench overlooking the cliffs, the ocean crawling beneath them and beating on the rocks.

There were moments when Alice thought her life was in a perfect, fragile balance.

She was... when she was honest with herself... absolutely head-over-heels in love with a sexy, tenderhearted man with madly talented fingers and fabulous hair.

Graham didn't ask what they were now and he never *called* her his girlfriend—not that he would waste any syllables for extraneous things like titles anyway—but she was visiting his room every night. And each afternoon that he could be coaxed away from the gardens. And every morning when she caught him on break, and when they passed on the paths...

Her bear, apparently, was insatiable, and fortunately, his lion was, too; however he protested that he wasn't going to be able to keep up this pace, every time she kissed him, he was more than capable of laying her down and making her bones turn to jelly.

They never talked about love, or the future. But Alice thought about a lot.

Love...

...and secrets.

There were also moments when Alice knew keenly that it was all temporary, that soon enough, she would be returning to her grubby real life, helpless to help her parents or her brother, unable to do anything to save either of them.

And Scarlet's shift form hung between them like a giant white elephant.

Alice was sure that Graham would tell her what it was if she asked, but she knew just as certainly that she couldn't ask. Forcing him to betray someone else's trust in him seemed like the cruelest thing she could do to him.

So Alice never mentioned how much help even a portion of fifty million dollars would be in their slow fundraising efforts, and she never brought up Scarlet if he didn't first, and she tried hard not to think about her life back home and the solution-less problems that she would return to.

Graham made it easy.

He told her stories about growing up in England, and she told him about growing up in the rural Midwest with her brother. He talked about his father, and learning how to garden on their estate when he was young. Alice told him about learning sports with her father, and fishing and boating in the rivers and lakes. He even told her, hesitantly, a little about his fighting days, and showed her a many-times-folded flier.

"King of the Jungle!" Alice chortled. "Look how short your hair is!"

"I could cut it again," he offered at once.

"Don't you dare," Alice said. "I think a guy with longer hair than mine is the sexiest thing ever."

He even let her work with him in the gardens at the top of the resort, showing her how to twist ripe strawberries off the plants without bruising them, and how to harvest herbs, and which weeds to pull. He told her what all the jungle plants were, and how they grew.

Evenings were often spent in The Den, sitting cozily with the rest of the staff in the living room, and over the course of the week no fewer than seven people later commented to her that they'd never seen Graham talk so much. Two of them had marveled over the fact that they'd never realized he was British before.

The glorious tropical days spilled one into another and Alice trembled, thinking how short their time left was.

"What's wrong?" Graham asked, taking a bite of his sandwich and giving her a sidelong look.

"I'm not ready for this to be over," she confessed quietly.

Graham was quiet. "Does it have to be?"

It was as close as he'd come to asking what they were going to do with the future.

"I don't know," Alice said miserably. "I wish I did."

Before them, the ocean wrinkled away to the horizon, dotted with a dozen small boats.

"I haven't seen boats out there before," Alice observed.

Graham squinted out at them curiously. "We don't often see a lot like that," he said, letting her change the subject without argument. "Must be some kind of fishing competition or something."

Alice might have tried taking the conversation to the topic of fish, but Graham's pocket abruptly buzzed and he withdrew his phone curiously.

The screen made him frown and stand. "I have to go," he said apologetically. "Scarlet said immediately, and she *never* says that."

He paused only long enough to kiss Alice—one of those kisses that left no sense in her head to worry with.

But the worry came rushing back as Graham disappeared in the direction of Scarlet's office and Alice gazed out at boats with her chest aching.

# Chapter 28

THERE WERE FIVE GUESTS waiting in the courtyard outside of Scarlet's office next to a pile of gigantic suitcases. They looked sweaty and winded and Scarlet was giving them a smile that Graham knew entirely too well: she was furious and frustrated and fighting very hard to give absolutely no impression of it.

"Please wait here a moment," she said with a polite nod of her head, and she clicked her way across the courtyard to meet Graham and draw him out of earshot.

"There a problem?" Graham asked with a growl. "You said you needed me immediately." He eyed the guests; they didn't look like the kind of threat that he had anticipated when he got Scarlet's text.

Two of the women were fanning themselves and one of the men, slightly overweight, was sitting on a suitcase like his legs had given out in the heat. The second man was the only one who was slightly menacing, and he was frowning thoughtfully at labels on the potted plants.

"I wish there was *only* one problem," Scarlet hissed. "But this is the most urgent. They aren't shifters."

Graham scowled across the courtyard. "Friends of shifters?" Scarlet had talked about relaxing the shifter restriction for friends of guests, especially for events like weddings.

"No," Scarlet said with a humorless laugh. "They don't even *know* about shifters. They are *furries*."

"Furries?" Graham repeated, confused.

"Humans that dress up like anthropomorphic animals. Those suitcases are entirely costumes. *Fur*suits."

Graham almost laughed.

"It was a last-minute reservation," Scarlet said defensively. "The charter has already left, and I can't send them back to the mainland on the boat until morning. We're going to have to put them up for the night. I need you to get the word out to the entire staff, and every single guest, that we cannot have anyone shifting in public, or talking about shifting, or doing anything only shifters can do, until we get rid of them. No magic."

She groaned then, though her posture remained perfect and to the guests she undoubtedly looked like she was simply having a nice, casual conversation. "And oh, Gizelle... will you find Conall, see if he can keep her out of the way. She's already on edge, the last thing I need is her getting scared. Make sure that Liam keeps the elders off the common grounds. We need to avoid a scene."

"What's our story?" Graham asked.

"That we're fumigating the hotel for an infestation of *cloth-eating* bugs and have no other openings. We're moving the existing hotel guests to cottages, and I'm having Travis quarantine the building. The humans will be put up on the beach for the night in a tent. In the morning, we'll have Travis take them in the boat to that new all-inclusive hotel on the mainland. On my dime, of course."

Graham winced. This was not a good thing for a resort already in dire financial straits.

But if there was one thing Scarlet was good at, it was guarding secrets, and Graham knew that she would bend over backwards to protect the trust of her clients.

# Chapter 29

NOT KNOWING HOW LONG Graham's summons would keep him busy, Alice took the empty sandwich plate back to the buffet and wandered around the center of the resort.

Amber and Mary were laughing and sunning at the pool while Neal and Tony were racing laps. Alice watched them a moment from the bar deck, considered joining them, and decided that she couldn't muster up the appropriate feeling of vacation for the moment.

"Get you a drink?" Tex invited, as Alice took a seat at the bar. He was sitting behind the bar tuning a battered guitar.

"It's probably a little early," Alice decided. "I'll take a ginger ale." Bubbles, she thought, but less regret. She had enough regrets.

Tex poured her a ginger ale from the tap into a glass of ice and resumed tuning his guitar. "Got a request?" he asked.

"Something happy," Alice suggested, eyeing his cowboy hat skeptically.

Tex laughed, touching the brim of his hat with a nod, and launched into a ridiculous song about faithful dogs and faithless women that had a fast, upbeat tempo, even if the topic wasn't entirely happy.

As he finished with a flourish, Alice's phone rang. She gave the bartender a thumbs-up and fished her phone from her pocket.

A glance at the number had her blood running cold.

"Are you okay?" she blurted, answering.

Tex busily turned away to do something at the far end of the bar to give her privacy.

"Jeez, Alice, you sound just like Mom." Andy's voice was reassuringly strong.

Alice gripped the edge of the bar. "You don't call unless something is wrong," she reminded her brother crossly. "What's going on?"

"You sound like you're a million miles away," Andy observed.

"I'm in Costa Rica," Alice reminded him.

"Oh, crap, I forgot. Is this costing too much? I wasn't calling for anything that important." Andy's voice was thick with guilt.

"No, it's fine," Alice said swiftly. "I have an international plan for the month. What's up?"

"I... I just got off the phone with Mom and Dad, and it's really hard to talk to them without really talking, you know. I can't tell them what's really going on with me, and it's all weird silences and waiting for the other person to talk."

Because they were keeping secrets from each other, Alice thought achingly. "Have you thought more about just *telling* them?" she prodded. If she could get one of them to break down, maybe the other side would cave, too.

They had one of the weird silences that Andy had described. "I don't know," he said miserably. "What if they freak out? What if they..."

"Spit it out," Alice told him.

"What if they think I... I don't know... deserved this?"

"Give them some credit," Alice said in exasperation. "They aren't jerks and they would never blame you for *getting sick*."

"They might not say it," Andy sulked. "But I'd always wonder."

Alice made a rude noise of exasperation that was probably lost in the long distance connection.

"Alice," Andy said hesitantly. "Alice, I know you've already done so much. You missed your last trip to Costa Rica because of me."

"My choice, Pipsqueak," Alice reminded him. "You don't get to make me a martyr, thank you."

"You said before you left that you might have a chance to get some money... there's a treatment I could qualify for, but I can't get the tests I need to see if I'm eligible without a down payment." Alice could hear the desperation in Andy's voice. "It's... about a grand."

Alice's heart dropped in her chest. "I don't have it," she said quietly. She wouldn't get it, either, she reminded herself. Scarlet's shift form, and the fifty million dollars it could bring her, was tantalizingly close—and impossibly out of reach. Her bank account was tapped. Her credit card was maxed. She wouldn't even have been able to come on this trip if her friends hadn't paid for most of it.

"Yeah, I knew that was probably the case," Andy said, trying to sound brave. Alice had a sudden image of him as a kid, chin quivering. She'd have done anything to protect him. She still would.

"So, what have you been up to?" Andy asked, in that determinedly cheerful voice he was so good at. "Meet any cute guys on your tropical vacation?"

Alice smiled despite herself, thinking about how far beyond 'cute guy' Graham was. "Oh, yeah," she said lightly. "I met my mate."

This silence was more shocked than weird. "What?!" Andy demanded. "Mates are a real thing? Who is this guy? What do you mean?"

Alice turned to see Mary and Amber walking up the stairs from the pool deck, waving as they approached.

"Mates are real," she told Andy. "He's a great guy, you'd love him, sorry, got to go! Losing the signal, whoops!"

She hung up on him, thinking with amusement that she'd just given him a great deal to fill the weird silences with the next time he called their parents.

"You ready for your big moment tomorrow evening?" she asked Mary as they came up to the bar with her and asked for water from Tex.

"It still feels utterly unreal," Mary confessed to her. "I can't even keep track of the days here, and suddenly, it's going to be tomorrow."

"The last guests are coming in on the morning flight," Amber said. "So, we'll do the spa tomorrow after lunch and everything else is already in place. Tony swears he has not lost the rings and checks on them every hour on the dot," she promised.

"It's weird not having anything else to do," Mary said. "I don't know what to do with myself. My last day being unmarried!"

Alice yawned. "I was thinking about a nap, myself," she offered.

"Were you busy last night?" Mary teased.

Alice grinned sheepishly.

"I could use a siesta before dinner," Amber agreed, rubbing her belly.

Mary threw up her hands. "Fine! Naps it is."

They finished their drinks and wandered through the cultivated greenery back to their cottages, Alice careful not to think of anything but how pleasant things were *now*.

She didn't need to borrow trouble from the future.

# Chapter 30

"OH, GRAHAM, THOSE ARE *gorgeous*. Even better than last week's! You've outdone yourself."

Graham grunted, knowing it was the truth as Chef picked up one of the tomatoes he'd just brought to the kitchens and admired its perfect, unblemished skin and bright color.

"These will be the crown of the meal," the cook said in delight. "Scarlet said there was an extremely important guest arriving in time for dinner tonight."

Breck, laying out the ingredients to stuff them with, gave Graham a suspicious look. "You wouldn't happen to know who, would you? She was very mysterious about it."

"Scarlet is good at mysterious," Graham said with a shrug.

Chef gave a booming laugh. "There's an understatement."

"Chet."

Magnolia was standing in the back of the kitchen, her violet silk dress swirling around her.

Graham might have thought he had simply misheard the cook's name, but Chef's face sobered instantly. Magnolia always had his attention in some measure, but now she had it completely.

"He's here," she said simply.

If Graham had not been looking directly at Chef, he would not have believed the number of emotions that could cross a single person's face in such a short time. It settled into something determined and apprehensive—a perfect match to Magnolia's.

The precious box of tomatoes was set down on the counter without a single second thought and Chef, in an unprecedented move, stripped his apron off and left it on the counter as he abandoned his work and went to Magnolia.

"You... spoke to him?" Chef asked quietly.

"I wrote," Magnolia said gravely. "When we were first trying to raise the money for the resort."

Chef bowed his head, slowly, as if he was fighting a great weight.

Graham was wild with curiosity by now, but trying to hide it. Breck had no such self-restraint. "Who are you talking about?" he demanded. "He, who?"

Chef and Magnolia ignored him. "Now?"

"He's out in the restaurant," Magnolia said softly.

"Have you seen him?"

Magnolia shook her head.

Chef rarely touched Magnolia in public, though his adoration was never exactly hidden and nearly everyone knew that they were mates. Now, however, he gathered her into his big arms and held her close. Graham could not have said if it was for his comfort or hers.

Graham could barely hear her fierce whispered words in reply, "He can't separate us now. He *can't*."

Then Chef was marching down the kitchen aisle, Magnolia gliding behind him. He left the kitchen, holding the door for Magnolia's regal exit, and the two together went out into the restaurant, hands laced together.

"I am mad with curiosity!" Breck admitted, and he dashed after them.

Graham considered staying behind out of respect for their privacy... for about three seconds before following Breck.

By the time they got to the restaurant, there was a small crowd gathered. Magnolia and Chef stood together, facing a strange man in a sharp suit who was flanked by a pair of uniformed bodyguards.

"Your Majesty," Magnolia said coolly.

"It's Your Highness again, Cousin," he replied, his voice equally chilly. "I stepped down from the throne." He paused, then said, "You look... well fed."

"I can still put you in a headlock, Einar," Magnolia said crossly.

"I don't doubt that you could," Einar replied, and Graham thought that the corner of his mouth twitched a little in humor.

Breck squeezed Graham's elbow. "Royalty!" he hissed in delight. "I knew Magnolia wasn't just anyone..."

"Royalty?" Graham hissed back in amazement.

"Valtyra," Darla said, appearing beside Breck. "That's Einar, he was the king of Valtyra. He recently abdicated in favor of his granddaughter and her new husband."

Einar's gaze turned to Chef, who was standing ramrod straight at Magnolia's side, looking grim and determined.

"Guard Chet," he said mildly.

"Your Highness," Chef replied, bowing his head stiffly.

"Oh!" Darla exclaimed quietly. "*Oh!* Chef is *Royal Guard*! This explains so much."

"What?" Breck demanded in a whisper. "What does it explain?"

"Royal Guard can't marry or have relationships. They forsake even their families and renounce their own happiness to serve the royal family." Darla's voice was pitched to carry no further than the three of them, and was full of compassion. She slipped her hand into Breck's.

"You're out of uniform," Einar finally said mildly. "To say nothing of delinquent of your post for twenty-five years."

Chef's face got very red and his mouth grew thin, but he didn't move.

Magnolia stepped closer to him, glaring at Einar protectively. "I didn't write to you because anything has changed. I'm not coming back, and I'm not leaving my mate."

Einar looked at her thoughtfully. "I wouldn't ask you to," he said gently. "I was wrong to, before."

That was clearly not the answer Chef and Magnolia were expecting; they exchanged wary glances.

"I was a young king at the time," Einar continued. "I thought I needed to toe the line, play by all the rules. You were supposed to honor the marriage contract and Chet was supposed to honor his duty. I took it personally when you chose instead to honor each other."

He held out an envelope, sealed with gold and red wax. "A gift from Their Majesties Signy and Kai Natt och Dag af Leijona, Chet. A full pardon of your absence without leave, a commendation for your service to the crown for the long and loyal protection of our cousin, and a complete and honorable release of your vows."

Chef took the envelope mechanically, looking dazed as his color washed away. Magnolia gave a little noise of surprise and covered her mouth, her violet eyes wide above her hand.

Then Chef was letting the envelope fall carelessly to the tile floor as he turned and crashed to his knees at Magnolia's feet as if he could not bear to wait another moment. "Agneta Annika Margareta Solberg af Bjorn, will you marry me?"

"I will," Magnolia wept. "I will!"

Chef surged back up to his feet, crushing her into his embrace and kissing her with less restraint than Graham had ever witnessed in him.

Einar grinned like a boy. If the bodyguards on either side of him were the slightest bit surprised by the sight of a giant cook kissing the king's large cousin passionately, they didn't betray a bit of it, stone-faced behind their sunglasses.

Magnolia was the happiest person that Graham had ever known.

She never met a day without a smile and her cheerful optimism had buoyed many people out of blue days. She enjoyed herself without limits, took pleasure in everything, and spread her joy like a small—or not-so-small—celestial body casting light into the darkness.

But Graham thought now that he had never seen her *truly* happy before.

Tears ran down her smiling cheeks as she kissed Chef—Chet—and laughed in delight and hugged first him, and then her cousin who had been king, and then, to their great discomfort, both of his guards.

Chef, smiling and crying, and not caring who saw, shook everyone's hands, including Breck's, Darla's—she stood on her toes and kissed him on the cheek—and Graham's.

Chef's happiness was only quieter than Magnolia's, no less.

Graham, watching them embrace again, suddenly found purpose, in a life that had been adrift of it.

He wanted to make Alice that happy.

It didn't matter where, or how, but he wanted to bring that kind of joy to Alice, if he could. He wanted—he needed—to make her smile like that, to weep in happiness. He would spend his entire life in pursuit of that moment, and if it were ever possible to achieve, he'd spend the rest of his life trying to do it again.

He slipped out of the restaurant through the empty kitchen—the rest of the staff had emptied onto the deck to congratulate Chef and Magnolia and ogle the visiting royalty.

As Graham took the white gravel path back to The Den, he stewed over his options... move to Minnesota, find a job... tell Alice what Scarlet was. He was willing to do all of it.

He was chewing over that last idea in particular when his lion growled near his ear and he looked up to see a figure standing outlined in the light of The Den beyond.

It was one of the human furries, he realized, just a moment before he registered the gun in the man's hands.

There was a sharp bite at Graham's neck that confused him a moment.

A dart, he realized, and he growled and clenched his fists. The man fired again as Graham charged him.

Graham's swing went wide as his blood seemed to turn to sludge in his veins. All his limbs were heavy. Too heavy. His second swing hit, but had no force behind it.

The man shrugged it off. "Save your fight for the cage, Grant," he sneered.

Graham was confused that he was somehow leaning on the man rather than hitting him. "Not... Grant..." he managed. Alice loved *Graham*. That was who he wanted to be.

Then darkness took him.

# Chapter 31

ALICE WOKE UP FROM her nap thinking of Graham.

This was not unusual. She couldn't seem to *stop* thinking about Graham: his hands on her skin, his growl, that devastating accent when he spoke, the pain and guilt in his gorgeous blue eyes, those moments when he softened and let his guard down and she wanted to crawl into his lap and kiss him... It felt like she was never not thinking about him.

What was unusual this time was the anxiousness that was coursing through her. Something was wrong.

Her bear was as bothered as she was. *He's not here*, she growled. *He's* gone.

Alice realized that she'd gotten used to a sense of him in her head, a comfortable feeling of Graham like a familiar scent on a favorite sweater.

Rather than letting herself linger in bed a few moments, touching herself and thinking about his hands, Alice rolled out of bed and pulled her jeans on, swiftly stuffing her feet into her sneakers.

"Have you seen Graham?" she asked the first person she saw.

Tex, at the bar loading a tray full of champagne glasses, grinned at her, but kindly didn't tease. "Last I saw, he was headed for the kitchen with a crate of tomatoes," he offered.

"Gotcha."

Alice took the stairs to the restaurant deck two at a time, the worry she'd woken to blooming in her chest.

The restaurant was in celebration mode; everyone was cheering and toasting and laughing.

At first, Alice thought it was just Mary and Neal's upcoming wedding, but she realized that it was far more widespread than that; the entire restaurant deck was centering their attention on a cluster of tables in the middle, where Magnolia and Chef were sitting together with a stranger in a fine quality suit. Dinner seemed to be an afterthought to drinking and talking, and most of the staff were mingling with the guests and drinking rather than serving them.

It looked like fun, and Alice was usually up for a footloose, impromptu party... but Graham was still missing from her head.

She lifted her chin at Mary, across the room, and turned away.

Graham wasn't here. Even if this had been his kind of gathering, which Alice doubted, she knew without hesitation that he was nowhere near.

She walked behind the restaurant, past the bizarrely-draped hotel; she had been warned about the fumigation deception to protect the shifters' secrets and knew about the accidental human tourists who were being put up on the beach. Travis had even fabricated something foul-smelling to give the ploy extra depth, and Alice covered her nose uselessly as she passed it.

The Den was empty, quiet and dark on the cliffs; no one answered her knock, and when she went in anyway, Graham's room gave the same answer.

If she thought he was in there, she might have opened the door and gone in without invitation. But her bear assured her he wasn't, so Alice left The Den feeling more mystified and worried.

Her feet took her next to the upper gardens, and Graham's close-guarded greenhouse.

She stood at the entrance of the garden a long moment, more hesitant to violate this space than she had The Den. This was Graham's place, his sacred space.

Alice breathed deeply, inhaling the scent of green things, fruit, and freshly-turned dirt. It was evening, and somewhere nearby a frog was trying to tempt a mate as the chorus of night insects began to swell.

Graham was not here, either.

She left the garden, closing the door behind her solemnly and stood for a moment.

The view from here was breathtaking. Alice could see down over the entire resort: The Den, the cliffs, the tented hotel, the festive restaurant, the cottages. The beach was a silver crescent in the falling twilight, and the waves wrinkled and flung themselves at the shore.

Alice squinted. There was movement at the dock and it took her a moment to realize that two figures were walking towards the resort's boat. No, one figure was walking, half-dragging the other. Someone had imbibed a little too much at Tex's bar, Alice thought, but after watching them for only a moment she knew she was wrong: the second figure was clearly unconscious.

*Graham*, she thought in panic as the first man dumped him unceremoniously into the back of the boat.

If he was unconscious, did that explain why she couldn't feel him in her head? She still knew he was there when he was sleeping.

Alice was already moving, running down the white gravel paths as fast as she could manage.

She had glimpses of the boat as she wove her way down through the resort and saw it slipping quietly away from the dock as she desperately ran.

By the time she got to the dock, the boat had already passed the reef and she could barely hear the roar of the engine over the sound of the surf. It didn't pull south and round the tip of the island, but headed north, and she stared after it in consternation.

Alice forced herself to think logically. If the boat had been going for the mainland, it would have gone the other direction. The only other place it could go was the abandoned installation on the other side of the island.

She set her jaw and bolted for the top of the resort, taking the steps two at a stride.

Scarlet was not in her office, but Alice went in anyway. Her bear's hackles rose at once; this was risky and they both knew it. She stepped behind the desk, wondering if she dared to actually ransack it for the keys she was after.

Before she could work up the nerve, a silhouette appeared in the doorway, tall and ominous.

"Can I help you?" Scarlet sounded as serene as if she hadn't just caught Alice creeping around in her office.

Alice braced herself for a fight. "I need the Jeep," she said, balling her fists at her side. She didn't phrase it as a request.

"Graham," Scarlet said, eyes narrowing. "He's... not here."

"The boat," Alice said shortly. "I saw someone dump him in the boat and go north."

Scarlet gave a sound that was half growl and half a sigh of great wind. "I can't go there," she said, sounding frustrated.

"I can," Alice said fiercely.

"You'll need help," Scarlet said, pulling a key down from a hook beside the door.

"There's no time," Alice said, reaching out her hand. The sense of urgency, of loss, was rising like a storm in her chest.

Scarlet was standing between her and her exit, the key closed in her fingers, and Alice started to bristle. "I have to go," she snarled.

Scarlet's green eyes drilled into her and for a moment Alice had to wonder what it was that kept the woman from the other side of the island, what could possibly be strong enough to resist that will and the terrible power behind it.

Before she could gather herself to fight the woman who was standing between Alice and her mate—however helpless a fight it might be—Scarlet dropped the key into her outstretched palm. "I care about him, too," she said simply, and stepped aside.

Alice was bolting before she could make any sense of that, key cutting into the palm of her hand.

The drive across the island was considerably less enjoyable than the same trip had been a week before. Gone was the cheerful comradery and the leisurely pace. Gone was the sunlight, and there was no laughter at Alice's lips as she pushed the Jeep as fast as she dared over the pitted road.

It took what felt like an eternity to get there and Alice could only stew over the memory of Graham's limp body being dropped into the boat and mourn the comfortable feeling of him in her head that she hadn't realized was her new normal.

The open gate to the compound caught her entirely by surprise and she drove in with more speed than she meant to; only afterwards thinking that she ought to have pulled the Jeep over and attempted some kind of stealth. There were lights past the house and Alice could hear unexpected music and crowd noise over the Jeep's engine.

Two guards suddenly loomed into the light of her headlights, bearing rifles.

"Ah, hi!" she called cheerfully, wishing she'd thought her plan through a little more thoroughly. She climbed out the Jeep, not wanting to shift and damage Scarlet's vehicle if she didn't have to.

Only then did she notice the two guards behind her, armed with nightsticks, and a chill went down her back; four guards was a lot even for her bear. "I was out driving around and got turned around in the dark," she bluffed. "I'm a guest at Shifting Sands, do you know how I get back there?"

They didn't look particularly convinced by her air-headed speech and one of the guards behind her suddenly said, "That's the girlfriend of the guy I collected from the resort earlier today. Cyrus is going to want this one for leverage."

One of the men raised his rifle and shot her.

For a split-second, Alice thought they'd shot her with a bullet and this was the end of her ill-considered heroism as well as her life. Then she realized that it had made a whooshing sound rather than a gunshot crack, and it was only a tiny sting of pain.

There was a small dart in her shoulder and Alice rationalized that it must be a knock-out drug. She was briefly amused at the idea of a dart meant for a human having any effect on her bear.

But when she reached for her bear, ready to unleash an angry, five-hundred pound animal on the unsuspecting guards, nothing was there.

She was still reeling from the realization when they closed in on her and her late attempt to defend herself was cut short with a staggering blow to the head from one of the nightstick-wielding guards. Before she could regain her balance, she was being bound and marched into the compound.

# Chapter 32

GRAHAM WOKE TO THE familiar sound of a distant, hungry crowd... and the loud growl of a nearby generator. He was lying on his side, darkened concrete before him, broken earth below him. It was bright, but after a moment, staring at his shadow, he realized it wasn't daylight; a brilliant worklight was trained on him. He lay still, trying to make sense of things, to figure out what felt so terribly wrong.

Alice, was his first thought, but he had no sense of her nearby. She was simply gone from inside of him, and the hollow place she'd been felt like a gaping hole.

He glanced down without moving and found that he'd been bound, at wrist and ankle, both anchored to the wall he was looking at. He might be able to break the chains as a man, but he could definitely break them as a lion... which was when he realized that his lion was as gone as Alice.

He must have made some kind of noise of alarm at the realization, because a boot found the small of his back.

"You awake yet, your lordship?"

Graham felt the hollow place inside fill with rage and recognition.

He rolled to the wall and brought himself up to a seated position. He was in a battered, three-sided concrete room. Bars had once enclosed the fourth side, but they had been burned and wrenched away. An extension cord snaked to a bright worklight on a tripod, focused on him. He felt like his limbs were heavy, and his bones were humming out of tune. "Cyrus," he growled.

"Surprise!" Cyrus gave him a toothy smile, standing well outside of the range of Graham's chains. One scruffy looking bodyguard stood just past him with a rifle in his hands. Graham couldn't be sure if it had more sedative or real bullets.

"You were a hard shifter to track down, Grant Lyons. Or Graham Long, as they call you now. Long time no see, *Long*." Cyrus laughed at his own joke. "Johnny Ace was very put out that you didn't want to pay his hush money. It didn't take him long to find another bidder."

Graham only grunted.

Cyrus narrowed his eyes. "I owe you, Lyons, I owe you a lot. You busted up my business real good, didn't you. And it's been real hard to get it started again. Have to keep moving around, doing shows in new places, building new audiences. I had a good thing in London, and so did you."

"There was nothing *good* about it," Graham had to protest.

"*You* were good," Cyrus reminded him. "Best fighter I ever had. Gave the crowd a real show, took a beating like a heavy bag and kept swinging. I would have made you rich beyond your wildest dreams. And you threw it away... for what? To be a gardener at a fancy resort where they treat you like trash?"

Graham nearly smiled. His life at Shifting Sands had been idyllic. He should have known it wouldn't last.

There was a chorus of cheers from somewhere not far from them and Cyrus grinned. "We're warming them up for you, Grant."

Graham got to his feet at last and could feel the sedative slowly leaving his limbs. There was still no whisper of his lion's presence or the slightest hint of his mate-bond. "I'm not fighting for you again," he said firmly.

"Oh, I think you are," Cyrus laughed. "You've gotten soft over the years, Grant, and you're weak."

"Unchain me and see how soft I've gotten," Graham challenged.

"Oh, you're still a fighter," Cyrus smirked. "But that's not what I meant by soft."

He snapped his fingers and a second, larger, bodyguard came from around the corner, a familiar figure stalking beside him.

*Alice.*

Her hands were bound, but only with rope. Her hazel eyes were blazing. "Graham? Graham, are you alright?"

"Does she even know your real name, *Grant*? I wouldn't have guessed that *girls* would be your weakness," Cyrus said thoughtfully, moving to brush her brunette hair back behind one ear. Alice jerked her head out of reach and glared at him.

Cyrus clearly decided that his fingers were worth more than making the point and turned back to Graham. "You never seemed particularly interested in the tail we offered you in London. Maybe they just weren't... large enough for your taste."

Alice went redder than she had been, seething.

Graham could feel the sedative burning off in the heat of his fury, but he held himself stone still, not wanting to tip Cyrus off.

A weaselly-looking man darted in from the opposite direction, a clipboard in hand. "How long, boss?"

"Not much longer," Cyrus said thoughtfully. "I'm not putting him into the cage until the sedative has worn off. That wouldn't be the show they've come for."

"We adding *her* to the roster?" the man asked with a raking glance at Alice. "She's tall and strong, she'd probably start a lot of betting."

"That depends on Grant here," Cyrus said, voice silky. "He fights... or she does."

It took every ounce of Graham's willpower not to betray the rage and agony his words woke. Alice, in a cage. Alice, defending herself against one of Cyrus' fighters. Alice, *hurting*.

"I'll fight."

The man scurried away again.

Was it the sedative that was keeping him from reaching his lion? Graham felt more himself with every moment... as much himself as he could be without the voice that had shared his head for so much of his life.

"Who are you people?" Alice demanded as they pushed her to the opposite side of the enclosure from Graham. "Why can't I hear my..?" She didn't finish, as if it suddenly occurred to her that they may not *know* about her bear.

"Can't hear your animal? Isn't that a nice trick?" Cyrus said smugly. "As well as providing us with this charming, isolated arena, Alistair Beehag had a whole arsenal of wonderful treasures that his nephew has quietly been selling on the black market. Oh, some run of the mill sedatives, poisons, hallucinogens, truth serums. But I was also able to snap up a good quantity of this particular drug—it forces a shifter to remain in their human form. You can mix it with a sedative, or administer it straight."

# TROPICAL LION'S LEGACY

Cyrus grinned as Graham finally realized what he intended to do.

It was going to be a do-over of his last fateful fight.

Only this time, he was going to be the one who couldn't shift.

# Chapter 33

ALICE WRIGGLED AGAINST the ropes holding her wrists, not exactly trying to hide her efforts, but trying not to be obvious. People in movies got out of stuff like this all the time. And if she'd had her bear...

She was so stupid, thinking she could just drive right up and save Graham single-handedly.

"One of these charming gentlemen was in the party of furries at the resort," she told him. "He recognized me."

"Yeah," Graham grunted briefly.

"I see that whatever they gave you hasn't made you more talkative," Alice said wryly.

"Alice," Graham said under his breath. "I'm..."

"I swear to God, if you apologize for getting me into this, I will kick you in the shins." She eyed the guards. "I bet they'd let me, too." Her voice gentled. "Graham..."

"I'll give you lovebirds a moment," Cyrus said, as there was a roar from a distant crowd and loud distorted music began to play. To the guards, he said, "Don't take your eyes off of them."

Alice eyed the guards, who were both holding rifles. More darts? Sedatives like Graham had been given? Real bullets? The lighting wasn't good; it was fully dark by now, and the blinding worklight was pointed at them, making it hard to see anything outside of their puddle of light.

"Alice..." Graham said again. "I love you."

It was a salve on the empty place inside her where her bear and the mate-bond had been. They weren't gone, Alice reminded herself, just silenced. She'd heard about the drug that made shifters stay human from Neal and Tony; it was temporary, it would wear off and they'd be back to normal.

"I love *you*," she replied.

One of the guards snorted in disgust and the other made a gagging sound. "Fucking shifters and their creepy *mates*," one of them muttered.

Alice squinted at them through the blinding light. "They aren't shifters," she said thoughtfully. "Is Cyrus?"

Graham shook his head. "Has kind of a chip on his shoulder about it, too."

"Stop talking," the other guard commanded shifting his rifle suggestively.

Alice subsided to silence, continuing to try to do something with the knots at her wrists without being obvious about it.

Before she could manage to do more than give herself mild ropeburn, Cyrus was back.

He stepped boldly up to Graham—much more boldly than Alice suspected he would if Graham had not been chained—and pulled his head to look directly into the light, checking his pupil reaction. "You're up next, your lordship," he said with satisfaction. "A battle to the shift."

"No..." Alice couldn't stop herself from saying. If Graham, like her, couldn't shift, that meant he had to win to live... and if he won... She remembered how he had looked at his hands, like they were stained with blood. He shouldn't have to do that again, ever.

Cyrus gave her a slow smile. "You'd prefer to fight instead of him, I suppose? Oh, you poor, stupid girl. Don't you understand? He loves this. This is what he was born to do. Has he tried to convince you that he's changed, that he's a better man now, that he's happy growing watermelons and mowing lawns at a luxury resort? He's no different now than he ever was. He still loves to hurt people. You can see it when he fights, how much joy he gets out of it."

Alice watched the guilt and doubt bloom over Graham's face, as hard as he battled to keep it behind his mask of stony anger.

"Don't do this," Alice begged, a note of panic in her voice. "I'll fight instead, if you want. I'm a wrestling coach, and I'm strong and fast. I'll give them a show." Could she actually hurt someone enough to make them shift, she wondered? Was she skilled enough? Did she have the resolve? If she could pin someone long enough, would they call the fight a draw?

Cyrus laughed. "Oh, Graham, isn't that touching. She's willing to take your place, the sweet summer child. Are you chivalrous enough to let her?"

Graham was staring back at Alice, his blue eyes like rocks. "Don't let her watch," he growled at Cyrus.

"You don't get to make requests, your lordship," Cyrus said, a hint of his own underlying anger showing through. "She'll get to see exactly what you are. She'll get to see how much you haven't changed."

Cyrus, Alice was beginning to realize, enjoyed pain the way Graham only thought he did. It was partly that he was seeking revenge for Graham's betrayal, but even more, he wanted the thrill of watching Graham *suffer*. He would enjoy Graham's torture: every bruise, every shame, and every regret.

Even after stories of Beehag's zoo, Alice had not really believed that such people existed. She looked back to Graham. She had not believed someone like him could exist, either: someone willing to draw a line of morality and sacrifice everything in order to prevent further horrors. Graham could have simply walked away with his winnings, and lived a comfortable life of freedom and never looked back. He didn't have to turn himself in to take down the ring, and he had known exactly what he was giving up when he did.

"How can you look at me like that?" Graham asked in a low growl, making Alice realize she was gazing at him with foolish fondness.

"How could I not?" she asked him, and when she smiled at him, his mouth cracked the tiniest bit.

They were not playing appropriately to Cyrus' need to see them miserable and tormented. Miffed, he gestured to the guards. "Unlock him, but keep him close. Bring her, too."

Despite her assurances that she could fight, none of them considered her a threat. Alice recalled her dismal performance with the heavy bag and her easy capture and wasn't sure that they were wrong.

# Chapter 34

THE RUINS OF BEEHAG'S zoo had been transformed. At first glance, it looked like a creepy pop-up rock concert, with noisy generators running massive lights and huge speakers currently blaring music. In the warm darkness, it was aggressive and challenging, and the audience—not big, but big enough—was cheering and drinking and betting.

The only difference was that instead of a stage, there was a cage.

It wasn't the burn-twisted remains of any of Beehag's enclosures, it was a shining new cage, probably boated in parts and assembled the day before.

While they were still outside of the glitter and spotlight, the guards gave Graham a pair of shimmering gold shorts and an ermine-edged purple robe to put on, and let him wrap his hands.

Alice watched with amusement that didn't quite mask her worry and despair. "I like how they expect you to beat the crap out of each other, but they want to make sure your delicate knuckles don't get hurt," she said mockingly.

She was so brave, so beautiful, so clever. Even dreading what she would think of the show, even knowing how this could destroy everything they had in so many possible ways, Graham was selfishly glad to have her there.

## TROPICAL LION'S LEGACY

She gave him... hope.

They were in an impossible place. Graham could see no way out of here; even if he won this round, Cyrus would pit him against another shifter, and another; he wasn't going to just let Graham and Alice walk away.

This was the dead end he'd always been ready for.

And somehow, against all reason, she made him feel *hopeful*.

Graham caught Cyrus glaring at him. Then the fight coordinator smiled coldly.

"You wouldn't want to start fighting without warming up first," he said with a smirk. "Boys?" He nodded at the guards, and Graham knew what was coming when someone grabbed him from behind and twisted his arms back.

It wasn't a fight, it was a beating, and a careful beating at that. The audience wouldn't want a rigged fight, they wanted the fantasy of fairness. So the blows were kept from his face, concentrated on his core, places that would cause damage, but not show bruises.

Graham didn't struggle; his only goal was to turn to keep the worst of it from Alice, who gave a wail of agony when it started and then begged Cyrus and swore like a sailor as they held her back. The pain in her voice was the worst of the torture.

When it was over, Graham caught his breath through gritted teeth. He had a broken rib, probably, and was glad it wasn't worse than that. He could still walk, and he could still fight, and that was what mattered.

Someone had a microphone and was shouting loud enough that they could hear it over the noisy roar of the generator.

"Ladies and gentlemen... are you ready? He's a seven-time event winner... The muscles with menace... Our very own angus shifter, Cinderblock!"

The shifter who walked into the spotlight, posing and raising his fists, was taller than Graham by a handspan and proportionally wider, built like a mountain. He raised a folding chair over his head and casually twisted it into a pretzel.

The crowd went wild.

Instinctively, Graham measured him as an opponent, feeling the familiar rise of adrenaline. Cinderblock was a big man, but he moved gracefully; his range of movement and speed weren't hindered by his strength, and he would be a tricky opponent even if Graham hadn't already been softened up.

Graham knew he ought to feel afraid, but the emotion welling up in him felt more like excitement. He knew what to do next, down to the very bones. It didn't matter that it wasn't fair, and it wasn't his choice... it was a fight he was ready for.

They were at the edge of the lit area around the cage, standing just in the shadows out of sight, very near the loud generator.

Past the crowd, the nearly-full moon was rising and movement in the sky caught Graham's eye.

"Let him say goodbye to his girlfriend," Cyrus said, loudly to be heard over the generator. He allowed Alice step forward to put her arms around Graham; she had struggled out of her bindings and one of her hands was free. The rope still hung from the other wrist, but the others clearly didn't consider her a risk. They knew that they only had to control him to keep her in line.

"Be... careful," Alice said, softly, as he cradled her face in his hands. She was blinking back tears, clearly trying to keep a brave face for him. "You aren't this," she reminded him near his ear. "You are *Graham*."

Graham kissed her without trying to explain that this was *exactly* what he was and stepped back from her, ignoring the ache in his side that had nothing to do with the broken rib.

One of the guards pulled her back when she might have tried to keep him from going and Graham had to turn away so he didn't try to jump uselessly to her defense.

He eyed Cyrus, who was watching him closely.

The crowd was beginning to tire of Cinderblock's showboating. The announcer, catching their mood, moved on to the introduction of Graham. "Out of the fighting circuit for ten years... the act you've been waiting for... one of the meanest fighters to grace the cage... lion shifter and lady lover... put your hands together for... the King of the Jungle!"

The crowd broke out in jeers and insults; Graham was clearly not the favored fighter.

They were expecting a slaughter, he realized, and he had to wonder if they were expecting it to be literal. The crowd at his last fight had had that same timbre, he thought. That same blood-thirsty lust.

Cyrus smiled slowly, savoring the moment. "Look at you," Cyrus mocked. "You can feel the thrill in your blood. You're still a fighter. You're still *Grant Lyons,* King of the Jungle."

There was another flicker in the sky.

"You're wrong," he said. "I'm Graham Long now."

"You're just the same as you've always been," Cyrus scoffed. "Graham isn't any different than Grant."

Graham smiled slowly.

"Except that *Graham* has *friends*."

Then a flaming dragon appeared above the arena, lighting the grass around the cage on fire and roaring a challenge to the crowd as it swept overhead.

Graham turned on the three guards who had been prepared to escort him to the cage, using their surprise to wrest their weapons from them as chaos erupted around them.

# Chapter 35

ALICE WAS LOOKING TOO hard at Graham to notice Bastian's aerial approach, but she was quick to take advantage of the distraction to grab the gun from the guard holding her. She might not be much of a fighter, but she knew he wouldn't be able to shoot anything with her weight hanging from his gun.

A bear, a panther, and a lynx stalked out of the darkness like the start of a bad joke and she cried out in warning, "They have Beehag's anti-shifting drugs!" She wasn't sure if they would hear her bellow over the sound of the generator.

Shots—real shots—scattered off a wall somewhere nearby as one of the guards fired wildly in their direction.

"And real bullets, too, apparently!" Alice added in a panic. She fought harder to get the gun from the guard she was grappling, and it ripped free into her hands. She swung it at the guard like a club, missed and nearly unbalanced. The guard, with more honed reflexes, recovered first and balled up a fist to hit her in the jaw.

Blinking stars of pain aside, Alice saw a charging deer of impossible size, followed by a pair of leopards, one silver and white, one gold and black. They didn't pause to battle any of the guards or shifters in fighting gear who were starting to gather; their goal seemed to be to clear a path for a human figure who was running behind them. Big bears charged after her, one polar bear, one big grizzly, and they bowled over the event staff that briefly attempted to stop them.

Alice wondered if the human figure was Scarlet for a moment, but then she was in the light, and it was the mermaid, Saina, ducking and dashing for the sound system.

Bastian made another sweep over the ruins, flaming above the heads of the fleeing crowd and the members of Cyrus' ring that were starting to muster a defense against the attack. Darts pinged off his hide and fell harmlessly to the ground below. The guard facing Alice was clearly having a crisis of loyalty, and at the massive dragon's second pass, broke off and fled with the audience stampeding towards the dock.

Some of the shifter fighters were taking animal form, meeting this attack with teeth and claws of their own. Was it loyalty to the ring, Alice wondered, or just that they couldn't resist a fight?

Then Saina had the microphone in her hand and the magic of her voice was falling over the crowd, calming them and settling a thrall over them. If they were running, they staggered to a stop. If they were fighting, they lowered their fists and paws and stood in a daze.

Alice felt only the slightest hint of it. At first, she thought it was because she was protected from Saina's magic by her dormant mate-bond. Then she realized that everyone in their immediate vicinity had shaken it off, Saina's siren music half-drowned by the constant noise of the generator and already spread thin over a larger crowd than she usually dealt with. Cyrus was bending to pick up one of the rifles, aiming it at the battle that Graham was fighting with the guards that had been escorting him to the cage.

Alice didn't know much about hitting, and she knew less about shooting, but she did know throwdowns, so that's what she did, driving Cyrus to the ground from behind.

He snarled and fought. Alice wrapped him tighter in her arms.

He headbutted her, smashing her nose.

"Foul!" Alice cried, tasting blood. She got her arm around both of his. "That would be a flagrant misconduct, asshole."

"You still think this is a game, Alice?" Cyrus hissed, trying to squirm out of her grip.

Alice clamped her arms down tighter.

# Chapter 36

GRAHAM'S GUARDS HAD been expecting a fight. They weren't expecting a dragon, or Saina's siren magic, or the ragtag team of animals that had shown up, but Graham's advantage of surprise still didn't last long.

It was three against one, and they were wearing light armor and carrying weapons; one of them still had a gun, and two of them had nightsticks.

One of those sticks came crashing into his broken rib and another struck his leg, hoping, no doubt, to disable him. Graham pivoted on the other leg and punched one of them in the throat, ducking a nightstick and coming up under the guard's arm at the elbow with his shoulder. The third guard hung back with the gun, trying to find an opening to shoot.

Graham didn't have to think about what he was doing; he simply acted.

Instinct and muscle memory took over, and he merely *was*: dodging blows, looking for openings, trying to keep someone between himself and the man with the gun. He wasn't Grant, and he wasn't Graham, he was just intuition and adrenaline.

Patience paid off; he was able to knock one of the guards into the other and use the ensuing moment of confusion to bring all his weight down onto onto the other one's wrist, thinking with an unexpected jolt of humor about his advice to Alice as it cracked beneath his assault. The guard howled and was out of the fight cradling his arm long enough for Graham to grab the other and spin, using the man's weight to build enough momentum to hurl him at the guard with the gun.

As they both struggled to keep their balance, Graham wrested the nightstick from the guard with the broken wrist and flew into them, knocking one out with a blow to the head and turning to face the other, just as a black panther materialized from the darkness and tackled him from behind.

Shots cracked out and the sound of Saina's lilting song suddenly went quiet as the generator failed with a sputter and a spray of sparks and all of the lights and sound equipment died.

The people who had been under her thrall shook themselves out, and, nearly as one, they turned to flee down the island for the dock. The guard with the broken wrist joined the flight through the sudden darkness and the guard under the panther cried out for mercy.

The panther shifted into Wrench and exchanged an amused nod with Graham.

"Thanks," Graham said briefly, looking around for a new opponent.

It took a moment for his eyes to adjust to the dim moonlight; apparently his lion's advantages were not all lost with his ability to reach his animal.

"Alice!" Graham cried, sprinting to where she was crouching. Her face was covered in blood and Cyrus, pinned beneath her, was snarling and struggling.

"I'm fine," she reassured him. "He'd be thrown out for poor sportsmanship if this were a real match. But I can't let him up until I have something to *do* with him." She grunted as Cyrus got a lucky elbow in her side, and adjusted her grip on him.

"I have something to do with him," Graham growled and he stepped on Cyrus' protesting head while Alice carefully let go of him, bending to pull the man to his feet when she was free.

"You going to hurt me?" Cyrus challenged, anger and defeat in his beady eyes.

Graham was more aware of Alice's gaze than he was Cyrus'. She wouldn't blame him for extracting justice.

But Graham didn't want to.

Of all the people he hated, as much as he desired revenge, here he was with every opportunity to give Cyrus back some small portion of the pain he'd lived with for ten years... and all he wanted was to be done with it.

He had wanted to step into the cage and fight a doomed battle at a disadvantage more than he wanted to inflict pain on this hateful, beaten man.

"No," Graham growled. "I'm not going to hurt you." He frogmarched the man to the dark cage where the Irish elk and the bears had herded most of the guards and fighters who hadn't fled with the audience to the docks below. Some of them were staggering in a daze that Graham recognized as Gizelle's handiwork and he wasn't surprised to see her tiny gazelle shape darting at Conall's heels.

Graham thrust Cyrus into the cage, not exactly gently, but not with the force that he could have. Someone had dragged in the guard he had knocked unconscious.

"You're not worth it," he said disdainfully as Cyrus stumbled into one of his unamused guards.

In the silence following the destruction of the generators, they could hear the distant sound of the boats starting to pull away from the docks below.

Neal, naked and grinning wolfishly, had an armful of chains and locks gathered from equipment boxes around the makeshift arena. "Is this all of them?" he asked.

Graham shrugged.

Tony, in tiger form, came circling around from the back of the cage and shifted back to human. "I checked the perimeter and didn't see any stragglers. These are the only ones that weren't smart enough to run for the boats."

Neal set to work securing the cage.

Bastian was back in human form and he was supporting a very wobbly-looking Saina. "What did you do to them?" he asked anxiously. "Are you alright?"

She had a shallow scratch on her forehead; Bastian frowned and reached for his first aid kit.

"I made them feel guilty," Saina said, with a certain amount of tired satisfaction, letting him fuss over her as she sank to a seat on a fallen speaker. "I reminded them that they were part of something terrible and made them feel bad about it. It probably won't last long—that's a lot more people than I usually try something so complicated with. I doubt it will last long enough for any of them to turn themselves in or rat out the ring; they'll likely forget about the whole thing and the island altogether by the time they get to the mainland."

She hissed as Bastian cleaned her cut.

"Are you hurt?" Graham asked Alice. There was an alarming amount of blood on her face, but it didn't appear to be flowing.

"Nah," Alice said dismissively. "I got a bloody nose and I might chew on the left side until I can shift again and heal up, but nothing that needs stitches." She gave him a suspicious look. "I'm more worried about you," she said softly, for his ears only. "They..."

"I'm fine," Graham said briefly. "Broken rib, maybe." He drew in a deep breath. Definitely a broken rib.

Alice made a little noise of anger and helplessness. "You should have Bastian bind that up."

"Darla's hurt," Breck said, coming out of the darkness with his arm around his mate, saving Graham having to argue about his rib.

"No more hurt than you are," Darla protested. "He got tagged with one of the darts and neither of us can shift now."

They had matching injuries, long slices on their arms. The runes circling their left wrists were gleaming slightly, reflecting the moonlight. Graham suspected that neither of them would have sought medical help for themselves, but Bastian solemnly cleaned the wounds for each of them and declared that they would probably heal with a shift or two once the drug wore off.

"Told you to stay back," Wrench said, frowning and folding his arms. If he'd taken any injury, it wasn't obvious on his scar- and tattoo-marked body.

Gizelle bounded into the space and shifted from gazelle to human in one swift leap. "I helped!" she declared cheerfully.

Conall, who had tossed a number of opponents easily aside in his Irish elk shape, gathered her into his arms. "I told you to stay back, too."

Alice gave Graham a sideways look. "You going to tell me that I should have stayed back, too?" she asked for his ears only.

Graham snorted, and his side protested keenly. "Wouldn't dream of it," he said gruffly.

"Let's see that rib," Bastian said to him without leaving room for argument once he had finished with Darla and Breck. Dragon ears must be as keen as a lion's.

"Great outfit," Breck observed as Graham reluctantly took off the purple satin robe. "Gold lamé suits you! You should add more to your wardrobe, m'lord."

Darla pinched him and said, "Ouch!" as she hurt herself as well.

"So, you're the King of the Jungle." Neal smirked as Bastian dug into his first aid kit.

"Don't they realize that lions don't even usually live in the jungle?" Tony asked drolly.

"King of the Savannah doesn't have quite the same ring," Bastian observed thoughtfully, unwinding a roll of cloth.

"Besides," Alice pointed out, "*this* lion lives in a jungle."

At one time, not so long ago, Graham could have imagined nothing worse than facing the staff with the truth of his past. Now, he gave a gruff laugh that turned to a hiss of pain as Bastian tied off the binding around his chest. Alice's hand in his tightened.

"You're going to have some good bruises," Bastian observed, his look suggesting that he guessed some of the other, less-obvious injuries Graham had taken. "Hope that Beehag's drug wears off soon, because shifting will do more for you than I can."

Tex had been guarding the van and he greeted them with a grizzly growl from the darkness. Everyone dressed swiftly and piled in.

The Jeep still had the keys in it, to Alice's comic relief. "Can you imagine what Scarlet would have done to me if I'd lost her keys?" she said, clutching her chest dramatically.

*Scarlet.*

Graham knew what he had to do.

# Chapter 37

THE JOURNEY BACK TO the resort was much slower than Alice's breakneck drive had been and the mood was lighter. Most of the staff packed back into the groaning van.

Alice, Graham, Breck, and Darla took the Jeep.

Graham gritted his teeth at every bump and pretended he wasn't hurting, but Alice knew better. She let Breck drive on the way back, content to curl in the back seat next to Graham, trying not to fall into him at the tight curves.

Scarlet was standing at the entrance of the resort, arms crossed, when they pulled in at last. She was frowning, to no one's surprise, but she refrained from quizzing them as they tumbled out of the vehicles and gave her the story in piecemeal bits and vivid, rambling description.

She frowned at a new bullet hole in the van, but to Alice's surprise, did not scold them for damage to resort property when she could have.

"That'll buff right out," Travis assured her with a grin.

Graham hung back, letting the others enthusiastically tell the tale of rescue and revenge with all the details they knew, and Alice stood with him. She felt like her bear was beginning to wake in her head and thought that she'd be able to shift soon. Her bond with Graham was a whisper in the back of her head and she was desperately relieved to feel it again.

"I'll have the Civil Guard collect the trespassers in the morning," Scarlet said dryly as the storytelling devolved into more and more colorful accounts of heroism. "I am sure you are all hungry and tired."

The others all tramped for the buffet and their mates and their beds, leaving Scarlet, Graham, and Alice alone in the courtyard.

"I trust you concluded your business?" Scarlet asked pointedly, not prying for details.

Graham grunted and shrugged one shoulder, then added, "It shouldn't be a problem again."

"I'm glad to have you back in one piece," she said mildly, with a glance at Alice. "Please don't let me keep you from food and rest."

Alice handed the Jeep keys back to her self-consciously. "Thank you," she said awkwardly. "For trusting me."

Scarlet only smiled her cool, distant smile and accepted them without comment.

Alice and Graham, hand in hand, walked through the courtyard and stood at the top of the resort looking down over it for a long moment.

At night, it was subdued, but no less magic, a haven of soft light in the darkness. Alice understood why Graham loved this place.

"Graham," she started to say.

But before she could speak, he was leading her away. Not to the buffet, as her stomach was hoping, nor to the Den, where her tired muscles longed to crawl into his bed again at last.

He led her past the hotel, still in its shroud, and up the path to his garden.

Alice had suspicions about what he had in mind as he opened the gate for her, but when she expected him to kiss her and pull her into his arms, he only sat on one of the ledges and pulled her down next to him.

"Graham," she started again.

"I want to tell you what Scarlet is," he said unexpectedly.

Alice felt her empty stomach clench.

"I... can't ask you to do that," she said mournfully. It was something she hated thinking about; every option was ugly.

"You are my mate," he told her simply. "And I don't want secrets from you. I... can't stand being so close to being able to help you and not doing it."

Alice gazed at him, alarmed and overwhelmed by the depth of what he was offering.

And she wasn't sure she wanted to know, because knowing meant she had to decide what to do with the information.

They were quiet a long time, Alice not sure if she wanted to beg him to tell her... or beg him not to tell her.

Finally Graham raised his gaze. "Scarlet's not a shifter."

He paused, to let that bomb sink in, and Alice stopped him before he could continue. "She's not a shifter? She doesn't have a shift form?"

Graham shook his head. "She's—"

Alice put a finger up firmly. "Don't tell me," she said firmly. "I don't want to know."

Graham blinked. "But..."

"I don't give a damn what Scarlet actually *is*."

"You could save your brother, your parents..."

"The guy with the business card? He didn't ask me what she *was*. He asked me what her *shifted form* was. If she doesn't have one… that's his answer. And it's an answer I feel just fine giving him. I'm not giving away Scarlet's real secrets, and I'm not asking them from you. I can give him the truth, and it doesn't… it doesn't feel like betraying Scarlet."

"He going to accept that answer?" he asked suspiciously.

"I don't know," Alice said merrily. "Let's find out! You have a phone in those gold lamé shorts somewhere? I still have his business card." Cyrus' men had frisked her, but hadn't seen any significance to the card and it had been returned to her pocket. She had memorized the number anyway.

Graham groaned. "Cyrus probably got it. I bet the cost of that comes out of my bonus."

"When was the last time you got a bonus anyway?" Alice scoffed.

They walked down to Alice's cottage to find her phone and disconnect it from the charging cable.

"What time is it there?" Graham thought to ask her before she dialed. It was still dark out, but dawn was starting to color the horizon.

"I don't know what time zone he's in," Alice said frankly. "And frankly, it serves him right to get a call in the middle of the night for being all scary and mysterious."

They sat together on the colorful tropical quilt on her bed, fingers twined, while the call rang through.

This was it, Alice thought. This was her brother's care and her parent's house and her mate's trust, all on the line with a stranger that she didn't know the first thing about. She thought about Jenny's ledger, creeping ever so slowly towards an impossible finish line, and what the money left over could mean to that.

She turned the card over in her hands. N. Padrikanth Moore was the most absurd name she'd ever heard, and she now counted a man named Wrench among her friends.

He picked up on the third ring. "Moore," he said simply, sounding cross but not at all asleep.

"Alice Anders," she said firmly. "You owe me fifty million dollars."

She was expecting to surprise him, but could not tell if she actually had. "You found out what Scarlet's shift form is," he said approvingly.

"Yup," Alice said.

There was a moment of silence. "And...?" the man prompted.

"And you owe me fifty million dollars," Alice said firmly. "I'm sure you know my bank account numbers and probably my passwords."

"What kind of shifter is she?"

"If I tell you, are you going to actually pay me?"

Alice couldn't miss the rich humor in his answer and she thought that was a good sign. "If you tell me the shift form of Scarlet Stanson, I will wire you fifty million dollars this very day."

"She doesn't have one."

Graham's hand squeezed hers and there was silence on the line.

"What is she?" he finally asked.

"Noooooope," Alice drawled. "That wasn't what you asked. I was sent to find out her shift form. I did that. It's not my fault the answer is 'nothing.'"

There was another silence long enough that Alice actually checked the connection.

She exchanged an anxious look with Graham.

N. Padrikanth Moore began to laugh.

Alice chuckled nervously, but wasn't actually relieved until he stopped laughing and, to her shock, said, "Very well, Alice Anders. You have technically kept your end of the bargain and I will keep mine. What do you want for the remainder of the information I'm seeking?"

"Don't have it, don't want it, won't do it," Alice blurted. "There's no price you can offer me."

"Everything has a price," the mysterious Mr. Moore insisted.

Alice looked at Graham, at the relief she felt mirrored in his face. "I think you're wrong," she said thoughtfully.

Graham slowly smiled and Alice felt her world fall into all the right places.

"It's been a pleasure doing business, Mr. Moore, I look forward to seeing your payment," she said, over whatever the man was trying to say. She hung up the phone and tossed it back onto the bedside table.

Graham's smile was like sunlight and strawberries.

"You want to make love to a millionaire?" Alice asked.

# Chapter 38

MARY AND NEAL'S WEDDING was simple and joyous... and completely lacking in battles, supernatural interruptions, and earthquakes.

Scarlet officiated, serene and solemn, with her red hair piled on top of her head, and Graham thought she looked soft and thoughtful, if a little sad, when Neal swept Mary into a passionate kiss at the end of the ceremony.

Alice squeezed Graham's hand, and when he looked at her, her eyes were dancing in anticipation and glee.

They all retired back to the event hall as night began to fall, for a reception where Chef seemed to feel he had something to prove. There was a groaning table of food and a five-tier cake decorated with animal footprints and real fresh flowers, topped with a plastic deer and a timber wolf stained reddish.

"Our supplier didn't have any red-maned wolves available," Darla said apologetically. "I had to improvise."

After the food had been enjoyed and the cake had been cut, Conall and Tex did a hauntingly beautiful guitar duet, and Lydia and Saina gave a salsa-bellydance fusion performance. Saina sang a song that set a glittering feeling of optimism and peace over the crowd.

Then Tony raised his voice and tapped his glass. "Your attention, please!"

Everyone found their drinks, prepared for a toast.

"Tonight is a night to celebrate," Tony said sincerely. "We are gathered here today in a place that been a happy ending for so many of us... and a happy beginning."

Amber smiled at him foolishly and Graham was appalled to realize he was doing the same to Alice, drawing his mouth back into a more customary scowl with effort.

Alice, her hand in his as naturally as if it belonged there, did not miss this and poked him in the side to make him smile at her again.

Tony continued. "We're here this evening in honor of our good friends Neal"—Neal's former Marine buddies all cheered raucously— "and Mary." Alice gave a cheer for her as if it was some manner of competition and she was single-handedly prepared to take on the entire platoon.

"I want to wish them a lifetime of happiness and love, and a full cup of laughter and joy." Tony raised a glass. "To Neal and Mary! Congratulations!"

Everyone raised their toasts and cheered, with scattered applause and laughter. Neal kissed Mary soundly. Out of the corner of his eye, Graham saw Scarlet rise to start the music for dancing, and gesture Travis and Bastian to start moving the chairs away from edge of the dance floor.

But neither of them moved, grinning back at her, and Tony went on. "We also have one more announcement to share, if you will all give me another moment of your time."

Scarlet turned back curiously, then looked to where Chef sat with Magnolia, perhaps expecting a formal wedding announcement from them. But Chef and Magnolia smiled knowingly back at her, which is when the resort owner seemed to realize that everyone was looking at *her*.

She returned her gaze to Tony suspiciously.

But it was Neal who stood then, grinning briefly at Tony. "I propose a second toast, to Scarlet, who has sacrificed so much for so many of us. She reminds us frequently that she is 'not running a charity', but time and again, she has put aside her own best interests to give us opportunity, protection, and shelter, at her own expense and considerable trouble."

At his words, many of the staff murmured agreement.

Scarlet frowned. "This isn't necessary..."

Neal waved her protest aside. "Words of appreciation fall short of the thanks we owe, so we have something a little more tangible to offer today. Jenny?"

Jenny was holding a folder as she stood and wove through the tables to where Scarlet was still standing.

"Scarlet," she said simply, "we know that the resort is in trouble, and that it wouldn't be if you hadn't gone out of your way to help us all. You took my sister and I in when you didn't have to."

"And me," Wrench growled from beside Lydia.

"And me," Neal agreed. "All of us from Beehag's zoo."

"It's my fault my mother is suing you," Darla added.

"Our fault," Breck corrected, an arm around her.

"You saved our retirement home," Liam said simply. The elders sitting with him gave murmurs of agreement, except Mr. Danby, who pounded on the table until Darla gently redirected him to folding and re-folding his napkin.

Scarlet gave Graham a brief, betrayed glare, looking conflicted. "I did what I could," she said quietly. "You don't have to—"

Jenny beamed at her. "We *did* have to," she said simply, almost bubbling over with happiness. She handed Scarlet the folder. "Shifting Sands will be yours."

Scarlet looked at her in confusion and slowly opened the folder as Jenny went on. "We gathered the funds from a variety of sources and we have raised the entire asking price of the island. Even if he wants to, Beehag's lawyer can't refuse the sale to Grant Lyons."

Scarlet's alarmed glance at Graham made him realize he was grinning again, and this time he didn't even try to turn it into a scowl. At his side, Alice laughed in delight.

He knew what was in the folder and had gone over Jenny's careful accounting of every penny: Conall's business had finally sold, and he pledged a massive chunk to the purchase of the island. Magnolia had liquidated a large part of the royal fund she had access to again. Laura and Jenny finally received notification of settlement of their life insurance from Fred's estate. Bastian had sold several of the more valuable pieces from his hoard. The survivors of Beehag's zoo had all wanted to contribute whatever they could, and their modest donations had added up slowly. Some of them had timeshare style contracts or profit shares laid out, but most of the donors had simply given the funds outright.

And Alice herself had promised forty-nine-and-a-half million (less her tax burden), thanks to the mysterious man with the business card. She had already confirmed the stunning sum in her bank account and Jenny had recommended a good accountant to help her handle the paperwork for the windfall and get her family's finances back in order.

Together, they had pooled enough to buy the island, buffer against Darla's mother's lawsuit, and keep operating for at least a few years.

Scarlet's face drained of color.

"All you have to do is sign the offer and express mail it to Beehag's lawyer," Jenny said coaxingly. "Graham—I mean Grant—has already signed his part of the contract, granting you full ownership. Shifting Sands will be yours, free and clear. The whole island."

Scarlet sank slowly backwards into her chair and she put the open folder carefully on the table before her. Then, to everyone's surprise, she put her face in her hands and wept.

There was an awkward moment of silence and Gizelle asked in a stage whisper, "Did you break Scarlet?"

Scarlet looked up at that, her face full of aching happiness behind the tears. "You didn't have to do this," she said again, choked.

"We didn't have to," Graham said, to everyone's surprise. "But we wanted to. You've done a fair bit for us that you never had to." He raised his glass of wine with the hand not holding Alice's. "To Scarlet."

The room raised glasses. "To Scarlet."

She closed her eyes a moment, more tears leaking down her cheeks, then opened them and reached for her own glass. "To Shifting Sands," she replied, and that received a chorus of echoes as everyone toasted the resort they called home.

# Chapter 39

GRAHAM'S BARE CHEST had been distracting, and his accent had been devastating, but Alice was utterly unprepared for the beauty that was Graham in a suit.

It was hard to watch the wedding, even harder to watch Tony's speech, and the emotional reveal to Scarlet that they had colluded to save the resort. Alice wanted to gaze at Graham only, to see the smiles that he kept trying to bury, to see the joy in his eyes, and his satisfaction at Scarlet's surprise and tearful delight.

"You know you could have kept the resort in your name," Alice told him, trying not to stare at the way his suit spread over his muscular shoulders as he stood to help move tables and chairs back from the dance floor. "It would be like being a landed lord again."

"I don't want to be a lord and I don't want to own a resort," Graham said with a shudder. "I just want to grow tomatoes and strawberries and let Scarlet deal with the rest of the nonsense."

Then he looked at Alice, his deep blue eyes intense. "And you," he added. "I want to be with you."

Alice's breath caught in her chest.

She couldn't deny the connection they had any longer, but they hadn't talked about what came next. "Let's go for a walk," she suggested, as the music struck up. This wasn't a conversation to try to have during the wedding chicken dance. Mary was too busy with Neal to even notice her skipping out on the reception.

Graham nodded, and he offered Alice one of his starched arms.

She took it, barely keeping herself from rubbing herself against it inappropriately, and they walked out along the side of the dance floor. Scarlet was circulating among the guests and staff, thanking each of them sincerely for their part, and she caught them at the door.

"My lord," she said to Graham. Alice didn't think that she said it in the slightest bit ironically, certainly not in the mocking fashion that Breck said it. For a moment, Alice thought Scarlet was going to bow or curtsy, but she only tipped her head respectfully. "There aren't words for what you've done for me."

Graham cleared his throat in embarrassment. "Scarlet, you've done more for my family... for this family... more for me... than I could ever repay. But it's not about debt or duty. This is your island. It's always been *your* island."

Scarlet looked between Graham and Alice, her face grave and grateful. "Thank you," she said simply, and she shook both of their hands in turn. Alice wondered afterwards if she imagined the tingling sensation that tickled up her arm.

She wasn't a shifter, Alice reminded herself, and she briefly wondered why someone who *wasn't* a shifter would invest themselves so deeply in a place made for them.

Graham and Alice escaped out the side door, leaving Scarlet to continue her rounds.

They made their way out onto the sprawling lawn, still littered with chairs and flower chains. The dais from the wedding was pale in the moonlight.

Without conferring, they walked towards it and stood looking through the archway at the sparkling ocean beyond.

"Alice," Graham growled, just as Alice cleared her throat and said, "Graham..."

"You first," he insisted.

Alice sighed, not even sure how to say what was bubbling up in her chest. She closed her eyes, and let the sound of the ocean on the rocks wash over her. "Graham, I love you."

Once it was said, it seemed the simplest, most obvious thing in the world. "I love you," she repeated. "I am a part of you, and you are a part of me I can't imagine being without."

Graham let his breath out as if he'd been holding it. "Alice..." he said achingly.

"I'm not done yet," Alice said quickly as she opened her eyes. "Graham, I want to be with you forever. It doesn't matter where, or what else happens."

Graham in a suit was breathtaking, but Graham in a suit sinking to his knees at her feet to gaze up at her in the moonlight was the most romantic thing that Alice had ever seen.

"I love you," he said, and Alice smiled to remember that they were the first words he had said to her. "I pledge myself to you," he went on. "Marry me, or don't, I am yours for all time, in all ways, all places."

She wasn't afraid of the words this time; happiness filled her so completely that there was no room for fear or doubt. "I am yours," she replied simply, and then Graham was flowing to his feet and pulling her into his amazing arms and kissing her with his amazing mouth.

It was several moments before coherent thought was possible. "Graham," she said, pulling away at last. "Graham."

"I will come to Lakefield with you," he said.

"I don't want to ask you to," Alice said. "I want to come here."

"Your job," Graham said reluctantly. "Your wrestling team."

Alice stroked his jaw, enchantingly clean-shaven for the occasion. "Do you remember when I told you that it's easy to be confused about the difference between loving what you do and loving to be good at what you do? That's the truth, and it's my truth, as well as yours. There are things I love about being a gym teacher, and being good at it is right up at the top of that list. But there's a lot I hate, like the administration, and the pay, and watching good students wash out, the parents..." She could have gone on for a while.

"But I'm a millionaire now," she said with a grin. "Or I was for a few minutes anyway. I don't have to teach middle school again if I don't want to. I'm not going to say there won't be parts I'll miss, but there are a lot of parts I won't miss, too... and this is an amazing tropical paradise. I'm sure I can find work to do here. Work that I'll love, even. Scarlet won't kick me out, and... you belong here just as much as she does. This is my home, now."

She wondered how to explain how much the resort was under her skin... she felt like it was the place her feet belonged, like she could do good here, like there was something about the island that called to something inside of her.

Something *good* inside of her.

Graham was smiling, that rare, beautiful, slow smile that he shared only with her.

"This is *our* home," he agreed, and he kissed her again until she was panting and clinging to him desperately.

"I can think of something I love to do," he growled in her ear as she started to work loosening the tie.

Alice chuckled. "Do you love it, or do you love that you're *good* at it?" she teased.

"Let's find out," he suggested.

"Your bed... or a strawberry bed?"

Graham didn't answer, but took her by the hand, and then they were laughing and running over the lawn in the direction of The Den... and the gardens beyond.

# Epilogue

GRAHAM RARELY ATTENDED the formal dances that Scarlet hosted most weeks; she didn't ask him to, and he didn't offer.

But Alice was adamant. "If I have to stomp around in those goddamn shoes for three awful hours, I'm doing it on *your* toes." It was the last dance before she and Mary and Amber and their mates returned stateside, just a day and a half before their charter flew out, and Graham thought that Alice felt guilty for skipping out on most of Mary's reception.

Alice planned to put in her notice at the school and pack up her things to come back to the resort, but the timeline for her return was still loose. Graham dreaded the weeks without her and would have agreed to worse than a dance to keep her close as long as he could.

It was no surprise to Graham that Alice was significantly lighter on her feet than she had advertised, and the feel of her in his arms more than made up for the snickers of the rest of the staff and the torture of having to wear a nice suit.

And Alice *liked* the suit.

Graham was beginning to suspect she'd only agreed to go to the dance to get him back into it.

"You'll excuse me, *my lord*," Breck said, appearing next to them as they walked off the floor at the end of a song. The waiter held out a hand to Alice. "Chef stole Darla for a turn around the floor, so I'm here to impart some of my wisdom to your lovely lady and show her how a dance floor ought to be used."

"I'll dance with you," Alice said, arching an eyebrow at him. "But if you add any wandering fingers to your words of wisdom, you'll lose them."

"I'm hurt," Breck said, pressing his chest. "You injure me by believing I would be anything but a perfect gentleman. My fingers have never gone *anywhere* they weren't invited."

"Oh, I've heard all about you," Alice said, letting him lead her out onto the dance floor with a smile over her shoulder for Graham. "And I know that Darla will be happier with all your fingers intact, so let's keep them that way, shall we?"

Breck's laughing protests that he was sorely misunderstood—and a faithfully married man at that—faded into the music as he led Alice out through the dancers to a clear spot on the floor.

Graham ducked his head, hoping to avoid eye contact with any forward women who might think this meant he was available for a dance and stalked over to where Tex was pouring drinks at the bar. Tex handed him a beer without being asked and Wrench, who was also clearly trying to dodge an arranged dance while Lydia glided around with one of the guests, clinked bottles with him.

Everything felt... practically perfect.

His mate was safe. His friends were safe.

The resort was solvent and they were going to own it outright, forever. They never had to worry about having it sold out from under them again, or losing the lease.

There were no secrets on his shoulders save one, and that was not his burden. His demons were laid to rest at last, and he finally felt wholehearted. He couldn't imagine loving anyone more than he loved Alice, or trusting anyone more completely.

"Who's that dancing with Scarlet?" Travis asked curiously.

"Haven't seen him before," Tex said. Tex had a bartender's memory for faces and stories.

Graham glanced towards the far entrance. There was a large suitcase and a fancy garment bag sitting by the door. "New guest," he guessed with a shrug. Sometimes dragons or other shifters who could fly chose to come in under their own power rather than taking a boat or charter plane.

"Good dancer," Wrench observed briefly.

Graham didn't have the best view, between the dancers around them and the distance, but Scarlet and the stranger were talking intensely. He couldn't gauge her mood from here, but it was clear that the new guest had *all* of her attention.

That generally wasn't a comfortable position to be in, but the stranger didn't seem to be the slightest bit intimidated, which was unexpected. He was actually smiling at her.

He looked... triumphant.

"Is he going to *kiss* her?" Jenny asked avidly, as the two came close together in a flashy dance pattern—much closer than Scarlet's partners' usually got—and paused longer than the music dictated.

"Does he have a deathwish?" Laura chuckled.

"Graham!" Alice hissed, breaking through the dancers with Breck in tow. "Graham, that's him!" Her hand closed around his elbow and she pointed in alarm at the man they were discussing. "That's the guy who gave me the business card! That's N. Padrikanth Moore!"

"Here?" Graham balled up his fists. If the man had followed Alice with some idea of revenge...

"Did you say *Padrikanth Moore*?" Jenny exclaimed in alarm, nearly choking on her drink. "You're telling me *that's* Beehag's lawyer? *Here*? *Dancing with Scarlet*?"

# Note from Zoe Chant

I HOPE YOU ENJOYED Alice and Graham's story! I have been waiting a long time to tell Graham's tale, and I was especially happy to have a chance to give Magnolia and Chef their own happy ending. I will be writing more of their backstory as a Christmas short – be sure to sign up for my mailing list or watch my Facebook page, as it will probably be available free on my webpage for a very limited time.

You'll find the answers to *all* the mysteries in the next book, *Tropical Dragon's Destiny*.

Read on for the exclusive short story, *Reunion*, in which Gizelle reconnects with Neal!

I always appreciate knowing what you thought – you can leave a review at Amazon or Goodreads or Bookbub (I read them all, and they help other readers find me, too!) or email me at zoechantebooks@gmail.com.

If you'd like to be emailed when I release my next book, please visit my webpage at zoechant.com and sign up for my mailing list! I also have a Facebook page and and a VIP group where I show off new covers first, and you can get sneak previews, chances at free books, and I'll answer questions you might have.

The cover of *Tropical Lion's Legacy* was designed by Ellen Million – visit her page at ellenmillion.com to find coloring pages of some of my characters and even signed bookplates!

# Reunion

NEAL GAZED OVER THE lawn, a slight smile at his mouth as he sat thoughtfully on the picnic table where he and Graham and Breck had shared so many meals.

It hadn't changed a lot in the year he'd been gone; though the hotel was no longer staff housing, it didn't look any different. The jungle still held proud sentry uphill, and the sun, high in the sky, beat down on the sunny lawn.

Neal closed his eyes. The air still had the same green taste and warmth, with just the slightest tang of salty seawater.

But so much was different.

*He* was different.

He'd found his mate, his reason for happiness. He'd made peace with his estranged red-maned wolf and reclaimed the life that had been stripped from him.

He hadn't returned to the Marines, though he'd reconnected with his teammates. Instead, he and Mary built their own life together, in the small town of Lakefield where she taught math to disinterested middle school students. He took his talents with machinery to a civilian job operating big equipment, and found satisfaction in working for a modest construction company, running excavators and graders.

It was a life he could never have accepted without his time at Shifting Sands, time he had desperately needed to put his ten years of captivity in perspective.

Neal opened his eyes at the sound of unfamiliar footsteps.

A big man, nearly as broad at the shoulder as Neal himself, was approaching the picnic table, stride determined. He was wearing an elegant silk shirt, perfectly pressed khakis, and expensive shoes.

Neal stood up, already guessing who this must be. "You must be Conall," Neal greeted him, remembering to look clearly in the other's face as he extended his hand for a shake.

Conall was Gizelle's mate, a famous classical musician who had built a small business empire in the wake of an accident that left him deaf. When Neal had first heard about him, he was deeply skeptical that such a man could in any way be a good match for Gizelle.

If Neal had been badly damaged by his years in a madman's menagerie, he could only imagine how it had been for Gizelle, who had been there longer than anyone could remember. For months following their release, she had remained in her gazelle form, and when she had finally shifted to human, she had no memory of her time in her cage, and she continued to be timid and traumatized.

Neal looked at Conall with thoughtful evaluation. He had not believed that a disabled man could possibly be what Gizelle needed, but his friends assured him that Gizelle had blossomed with this man's love, and was more calm and centered than anyone had ever imagined she could be.

Scarlet had kept him apprised of Gizelle's status, but her emails were brisk and impersonal, much like she was. Graham and Breck, no surprise, had not proved to be good correspondents. There had been a lot to catch up on in person, and they had been quick to assure him that Gizelle was happy and well.

Neal had to take that on faith, as Gizelle had been avoiding him since his return to the resort.

"You're Neal," Conall replied, and Neal thought his gaze was as suspicious as Neal's had been. "It's good to meet you."

His handshake was strong, his fingers calloused. He had fine clothing and a haughty tilt to his broad jaw.

They assessed each other for a long moment after they reclaimed their hands

"I've heard a lot about you," Neal said, self-conscious about the shape of his mouth as he spoke; Conall had to lip-read his words without Gizelle to help him hear.

"I've heard a lot about you," Conall echoed him with challenge. After a moment, he added, more gently, "Thank you."

Neal was surprised. "For what?"

"For your part in the liberation of the zoo," Conall explained. "For helping Gizelle feel safe again. She is very fond of you, and she missed you when you left." He spoke grimly, matter-of-factly.

He might have been jealous, Neal thought, or protective. Either would be understandable. "I'd like to see her before we leave," Neal said with a neutral nod. "If she wants to."

"She does," Conall said with a similar nod. "It just takes her a little while to work up to things sometimes." He said it with warm patience that put Neal's last reservations to rest. This was a man who understood Gizelle, who was willing to accommodate her quirks and love her for all her unique characteristics, not just in spite of them.

"Whenever she's ready," Neal agreed. "I... missed her, too." The two of them had been the last of the zoo to leave the island; that alone would have given them a bond. The shy gazelle had been Neal's real remaining tie to the resort, and he never would have left if it hadn't been to follow his own mate to another life. He sometimes felt guilty for leaving Gizelle behind, knowing how hard her trust was to win and worrying that he had betrayed it with his departure.

Conall frowned at Neal's mouth and then seemed to understand, giving a crisp nod.

It was tricky ground to navigate; admitting fondness for another man's mate was not particularly straightforward, and it was burdened by social norms that simply didn't apply. Neal had to trust that Conall would realize that their affection was platonic, as Mary did.

"So, ah, how are you liking Shifting Sands?" he asked, recognizing a place for small talk.

"Hard to complain," Conall replied briefly. "Er, looking forward to your wedding?"

"I am," Neal said, and it was true. There was something satisfying about the idea of standing up in front of their friends to make the bond that he and Mary had official. "It would mean a lot if you and Gizelle were there." He was sure that Mary had distributed invitations, but it seemed polite to invite Conall in person since he was there.

Conall looked at him quizzically for long enough that Neal wondered if he would have to repeat himself, then nodded. "I think we will be there, but it's always hard to predict."

Neal laughed, and Conall cracked a smile.

"Thank you," Neal said sincerely. Then he impulsively added, "Thank you for taking care of her."

Their second handshake was considerably more friendly than the first, and Neal caught himself thinking that he could like this man, given time.

It was too bad he was leaving in just two weeks. Time was the one thing they didn't have.

---

"I HAVEN'T BEEN RUNNING!" Gizelle blurted, when Neal finally encountered her, nearly a week later, just a day before the wedding.

She was standing at the steps to the beach holding two kittens that didn't want to be held. A fluffy gray half-grown cat with white paws was squirming under one arm, while its sleeker, cream-colored companion had all four paws on Gizelle and was pushing out against her opposite arm with stiff, determined legs.

"It's good to see you," Neal said mildly, walking up the steps with his towel folded under his arm.

She was, as he had been warned, very different looking than the woman who had been a gazelle for so much of their friendship.

She still had wild, white streaks in her wavy dark hair, but it was back in a braid now. It wasn't a particularly tidy braid, but it was out of her face, and she didn't seem uncomfortable in her sundress. She moved less timidly, and she wasn't trembling, or looking for escape. She was still thin, but her cheeks were not as hollow and her brown eyes seemed less haunted.

The gray kitten had oozed itself out of her arms so that only the back legs were still hooked around Gizelle's elbow, body and head hanging down as she stretched white paws towards freedom. Gizelle shifted her grip, trying to gather both cats together.

The cream-colored kitten had orange Siamese points, and yowled accurately to the breed as it struggled gamely against the indignity.

Gizelle gently tucked paws and tails back into the crook of her elbow. The gray one started purring in defeat. The cream kitten struggled in earnest but Gizelle gently hung on. "These are my Christmas kittens," she explained to Neal. "The angry one is Tyrant and the other is The Sweet One."

"It's nice to meet you," Neal said politely to the put-out, half-grown cats. "Where are you taking them?"

"There are humans on the beach," Gizelle explained. "They don't have animals in them, but Scarlet says that doesn't make them bad people."

"I heard," Neal said; he'd been warned not to shift or do anything in front of the unexpected strangers that might cause them suspicion. He wondered what that had to do with the kittens.

A terrible thought occurred to him, confirmed when Gizelle went on.

"I thought I would see if they wanted voices," she said cheerfully. "Because the kittens don't have humans inside of them, and maybe they are lonely."

Neal blinked at her. "You... can't just mash them together into one body," he said, as gently as he could. "It doesn't work that way."

"Are you sure?" Gizelle asked skeptically.

"Positive," Neal assured her.

Gizelle wilted. "It seems like it *ought* to work that way," she said, sulky.

"Anyway, wouldn't you miss your kittens, if you gave them away?" Neal said, hoping he didn't sound too desperate.

Gizelle snuggled them both closer, to squawks of protest. "Yes," she admitted. "But Tyrant is more Scarlet's than mine anyway. Everyone thinks that's very funny except Scarlet."

She sat down on the steps and pulled Tyrant back down from the shoulder she was trying to scale. "Scarlet also said I shouldn't bother the human people," she said, sounding guilty.

Neal sat beside her. "It's probably not a good idea," he said sympathetically. "They don't know about shifters, and they might be frightened."

"Do you know, when we met, I thought you didn't have a voice at first?" Tyrant was trying to bolt over Gizelle's shoulder again, and was tugged gently back to the young woman's lap. "Your wolf was so far away, so quiet."

That wasn't the case anymore, and Neal's red-maned wolf chuckled in his head.

"He's made up for lost time," Neal said wryly.

*As if I was the chatty one in this partnership*, his wolf said snidely.

Neal waited to see if Gizelle would have anything to say about the comment; he'd heard from Breck that she could hear shifters' animal voices.

But she only gave him a shy sideways look. "I'm getting better at people," she said hopefully. "People with voices, anyway."

"So I've heard," Neal said warmly. "Everyone is so proud of you."

That seemed to please her.

Tyrant gave a final, frantic squirm for freedom and Gizelle let her go. The kitten bolted away across the broad step, groomed her tail angrily, and then sauntered away as if nothing in the world was wrong. Sweet One remained in Gizelle's arms, purring, and the gazelle shifter stroked her gently and tickled her face.

"I missed you," Gizelle said sheepishly to her lap, but Neal knew she wasn't talking to the cat. "I was lost for a while."

"I was sorry to leave," Neal said gently. "But it was time for me to go. I needed to get back out into the world, take back my life, be with my mate."

"I know," Gizelle said eagerly, looking up at him. "I know now! I have a mate, too. He's so splendid and amazing. Have you met him?"

Neal smiled at her. "I liked him," he said approvingly. "And I'm so happy for you."

Her face unexpectedly fell. "I gave him the lock to your cage," she said anxiously. "It was Christmas, and I hope you aren't angry."

"Of course not," Neal told her swiftly. "It was yours to give."

The relief across her face was like sunlight after a storm.

"I thought you might be mad," she said honestly. "But it was the only thing I had."

"It was a beautiful gift," Neal assured her. "Conall must have appreciated it very much."

"Yes," Gizelle said simply. "Because I gave it to him."

Her eyes were just as Neal had remembered, wise and full of hope, but there was less fear in them now, he thought.

To his surprise and Sweet One's discomfort, Gizelle leaned forward then and wrapped her arms around him for a swift hug, her head for a moment on his collarbone. "I have something else to give you," she said, releasing him almost immediately. Sweet One escaped her lap and groomed herself lazily on the step below them.

"You don't have to give me anything," Neal assured her.

"I do," Gizelle said firmly. "Otherwise you will die."

Then she gazed at him sternly, and he blinked, and she was standing up. "Chef has something delicious for dinner tonight," she said easily, as if she had not just announced Neal's potential death. "But no one will eat it."

"What did you want to give me?" Neal asked, deeply confused as he stood with her. Sweet One was nowhere to be seen.

"I already did," Gizelle said patiently.

"You said I would die," Neal reminded her.

"But you didn't, did you," Gizelle pointed out.

"I... suppose not?"

Then Gizelle hugged him a second time. "Thank you for coming back," she said softly. "I may not need you anymore, but I still missed you. You were my first friend."

Neal carefully put his arms around her in return. "You helped me back every bit as much as I helped you," he said gratefully, giving her a quick squeeze and releasing her. It was a far cry from the first tentative touch of her gazelle's whiskers.

Gizelle stepped back and smiled up at him. "That's what friends do," she said confidently.

"Will you come to our wedding tomorrow?" Neal asked. "Did you get the invitation?"

"It had frosting you couldn't lick," Gizelle said eagerly. "Like sugar, but sharp." Her face went thoughtful. "I don't know if I came to it or not. It isn't long now."

"It's tomorrow," Neal reminded her. "In the evening."

"No, it's a little longer than that," Gizelle insisted. "But not much."

Neal suspected they were not talking about the same thing. "The wedding?" he clarified.

"No," Gizelle said with an oddly sad smile. "The end."

"The end of... what?"

"Of me. Of everything." Her hands were shaking, and as soon as she realized it, Gizelle tucked them into fists and put them behind her, smiling fiercely. "Nevermind," she said swiftly. "It's quiet *now*. I *will* come to your wedding. I *did* carry flowers for Darla."

"Do you want to carry flowers for us?" Neal asked, not at all sure what to make of her doomsaying. He was pretty sure he shouldn't take her literally.

"I'll ask Graham!" Gizelle said enthusiastically, which Neal had to take as a *yes*.

Then she was gone, flying away on fleet, bare feet.

Neal was still shaking his head when he returned to the cottage he was sharing with Mary.

"Did you finally catch up with Gizelle?" she asked at once, perhaps sensing his bemusement as he laid a kiss on her head.

"She's come a long ways," Neal said. The Gizelle who had first transformed to save him would never have given a willing hug, let alone two of them.

"She tried to explain to me that Jenny was the one who taught her how to shift when I finally saw her yesterday," Mary said, putting aside her book. "What did you two talk about?"

Neal laughed. "I think she has a skewed sense of causality," he observed. "She also seemed to think she just saved my life."

Mary pulled him down to kiss her. "Then I owe her a great debt of gratitude," she purred in his ear. "Because you've got somewhere to be tomorrow, and I'd hate to have to marry a corpse."

"That could be... messy," Neal agreed with a chuckle. "Depending on the method of death. And we paid a lot for the suit."

They shared a long, lingering kiss that somehow ended up with both of them wedged uncomfortably into a chair that barely held Neal alone.

"I can't wait to share the rest of my life with you," Mary sighed, as they untangled their limbs and pried themselves out the wicker chair.

"Can you wait until we get to the bed?" Neal teased.

Mary kissed him in answer, and they only just made it there.

It was only much later that Neal remembered Gizelle's odd prediction and wondered what she meant by the end that was coming...

# More Paranormal Romance by Zoe Chant

*DANCING BEARFOOT.* (**Green Valley Shifters # 1**). A single dad from the city + his daughter's BBW teacher + a surprise snow storm = a steamy story that will melt your heart.

*Bodyguard Bear.* (**Protection, Inc. # 1**). A BBW witness to a murder + the sexy bear shifter bodyguard sworn to protect her with his life + firefights and fiery passion = one hot thrill ride!

*Bearista.* (**Bodyguard Shifters # 1**). A tough bear shifter bodyguard undercover in a coffee shop + a curvy barista with an adorable 5-year-old + a deadly shifter assassin = a scorching thrill ride of a romance!

*Firefighter Dragon.* (**Fire & Rescue Shifters # 1**). A curvy archaeologist with the find of a lifetime + a firefighter dragon shifter battling his instincts + a priceless artifact coveted by a ruthless rival = one blazing hot romance!

*Royal Guard Lion* A curvy American shocked to learn that she's a lost princess + a warrior lion shifter sworn to protect her + a hidden shifter kingdom in desperate need of a leader = a sizzling romance fit for a queen!

# Zoe Chant on Audio

***DANCING BEARFOOT** – **Audiobook*** - A single dad from the city + his daughter's BBW teacher + a surprise snow storm = a steamy story that will melt your heart.

***Kodiak Moment** – **Audiobook*** - A workaholic wildlife photographer + a loner bear shifter + Alaskan wilderness = one warming and sensual story.

***Hero Bear** - **Audiobook*** - A wounded Marine who lost his bear + a BBW physical therapist with a secret + a small town full of gossips = a hot and healing romance!

# Zoe Chant, writing under other names

***RAILS; A NOVEL OF TORN World*** by Elva Birch. License Master Bai knows better than to dream about his Head of Files, Ressa. A gritty and glamorous steampunk-flavored novel of murder, sex, unrequited love, drugs, prostitution, blackmail, and betrayal.

*Laura's Wolf* (**Werewolf Marines # 1**), by Lia Silver. Werewolf Marine Roy Farrell, scarred in body and mind, thinks he has no future. Curvy con artist Laura Kaplan, running from danger and her own guilt, is desperate to escape her past. Together, they have all that they need to heal. A full-length novel.

*Mated to the Meerkat*, by Lia Silver. Jasmine Jones, a curvy tabloid reporter, meets her match in notorious paparazzi and secret meerkat Chance Marcotte. A romantic comedy novelette.

*Handcuffed to the Bear (Shifter Agents # 1)*, by Lauren Esker. A bear-shifter ex-mercenary and a curvy lynx shifter searching for her best friend's killer are handcuffed together and hunted in the wilderness. Can they learn to rely on each other before their pasts, and their pursuers, catch up with them? A full-length novel.

*Keeping Her Pride (Ladies of the Pack # 1)*, by Lauren Esker. Down-and-out lioness shifter Debi Fallon never meant to fall in love with a human. Sexy architect and single dad Fletcher Briggs has his hands full with his adorable 4-year-old... who turns into a tiny, deadly snake. Can two ambitious people overcome their pride and prejudice enough to realize the only thing missing from their lives is each other?

Made in the USA
Coppell, TX
26 October 2019